Mermaid Eclipse

N.E. CARLISLE

outskirts
press

Outskirts Press, Inc.
http://www.outskirtspress.com

ISBN: 978-1-9772-2772-0

Library of Congress Control Number: 2020910014

Cover Photo © 2020 Lori Hammond. All rights reserved - used with permission.

Outskirts Press and the "OP" logo are trademarks belonging to Outskirts Press, Inc.

PRINTED IN THE UNITED STATES OF AMERICA

To my mom and dad who gave me the confidence to dream.

Contents

Chapter 1

I waded toward the rocks, my vision obscured by sand flies feasting on a mollusk. This angled spot protected from the intense waves crashing toward the shore was half high beach rock and half hidden earth submerged in the depths near the edges of a small sinkhole. I knew this place and was careful to not step in the hole but to move my body, shuffling my feet around it. Stingrays inhabited these pockets of sand where I found my footing. One experience with a barb thrust into your foot, ankle, leg, or other body part would keep the timid from these waters, and the rest of us learned to be cautious. I wasn't a fan of the beach itself. I knew it was just a portal that all of us needed to enter these wild waters, and many were happy to rest in the sun on the warm moldable reminder that it was not quite earth—it was made of all the stuff the ocean had to offer and at high tide was reclaimed and returned to the sea.

When we were toddlers, my parents took my brother and me to build sandcastles and play in the surf. I would scream and refuse to walk on the sand. The gritty texture sliding between my toes was more than I could handle. The salty spray of the ocean disturbed my senses and made my skin sting. The constant back and forth of the waves and the shifting tide were unsettling. The ocean made me cry. It was the beginning of people judging my subtle peculiarities, or I what I prefer to call my personality. That I am a twin made the differences important. My parents had an expectation, and they brought me daily to the beach. Since it bothered me so much, in their minds it meant that I needed to persevere and become desensitized. I often wondered—if I had been born solo, would anyone have noticed my meltdowns as unusual or would they have merely wiped off that sand between my toes, given me a kiss, and taken me home? I would never know, because evidently I was the odd twin. I felt blessed that my twin was a boy and I was a girl—even though people, or as I refer to them, morons—still asked my mother if we were identical twins. My mother calmly responded, "No, one of them has a penis—they're fraternal twins."

Morgan, my brother, was a strapping, hearty boy—people liked to comment on his athleticism and rugged good looks. His hair was dark with soft curls, like my mother's. People stopped and commented on his hair. He always disliked that it was curly. He wanted straight hair like my father's and never understood its value or why people stopped him on the street or why it tempted some to run their fingers through it. He was attractive, and I wished I had his curly hair, but other than that—he was just okay. He did what he did, but I wasn't impressed, for sure. Basically, he took up too much room in my life. He hogged all the oxygen in the womb and never stopped. Now I was afraid he wouldn't have any oxygen as I scanned the waters for that curly head of hair and the rest of him. I could see only his surfboard floating toward shore.

My talented and creative, yet not so wise, parents gave us matching letter names—Muriel and Morgan. I'm not sure if it was out of convenience or necessity, but we were always in the same classes at school and in the same after-school activities. When we were younger, we were "The Twins"—then, as we grew older, other nicknames emerged. Everyone tried the M&M candy references with us—the irony being we're allergic to peanuts and tree nuts, food dyes, and anything else that might taste good in the popular candy. We frequently flirted with anaphylaxis.

I left my rocky vantage point and swam toward the board. I saw him caught in a riptide and swimming out of it, but then he went under. So you might wonder—if I hated the beach so much, why was I here on this too-sunny day, watching my brother surf? Ahh, that's an easy answer: It's because I adored my cousin Brooke. She was here, catching waves. Other than the beautiful fact that her name starts with another letter of the alphabet (than M), she was that perfect combination of grace and skill.

Even when she wiped out, you'd think "I wish I did that!" When she surfed, I braved the uncomfortable grittiness and took pleasure in watching her dance between the waves. Morgan made surfing look like work, and honestly I was in a constant state of stress when he was out there. I didn't want to find out when a shark ate him or when the board crashed into his head whether I would be empathetic (literally feeling the pain). I suspected an eerie twin thing between us, but more so on his part. He almost always knew when I was in some trouble or sick. Me—not so much. The bottom line was I didn't want to find out what it was like not being a twin.

Dark-gray clouds cast a shadow over the rest of the surfers. This was when I experienced the draw of the sea and the landscape. It was in these dark moments when I felt like it might rain that I wanted to leap from my usual blanket on the shore and join them. Today I was in it, and the wind blew the clouds out past the boards and swimmers, letting the sun peek boldly out, guiding me to his board. Brooke spotted me and Morgan's board. I reached for his board and she shouted at me: "He's already in. He just lost the board."

I swam his board in. On shore, came the part I never liked. She rushed up, as always, board close to her body, and shook her hair—like a dog after a bath—getting me wet.

"Hey, Muri! Glad you came out."

I spotted Morgan down the beach resting in the sand, catching his breath. I tried to hide the panic I felt as his board floated in the water without him.

I turned to Brooke. "Yeah, I wanted to connect and make sure you realized we're being abducted against our will over the long weekend—forced to go camping as a family. Please come...please!" I dropped Morgan's surfboard. Brooke took off her wetsuit and grabbed a snack from her nearby satchel.

"Nah—you guys will have fun. Your family doesn't go anywhere. It'll be good for you. Anyway, the last time I went camping it was with my mom. Not happening."

I felt the cringe on my face and the awkward tingles traveling up my neck. Her mom was dead. My dad and her mom were siblings and the driving force behind any Lutey camping trip. That was our last name: Lutey. Brooke's last name was Kainoa, which was ever so much cooler than ours. Her mom kept the maiden name Lutey. I would have ditched my name in a heartbeat. Muriel Lutey—just not good baby-naming, folks. Now Brooke Kainoa, that's a name. Her dad was Hawaiian and had Brooke on a surfboard before she could walk. She moved here after her mother died two years ago. She'd tried to get me to surf every day that she was out there. I just couldn't do it. I knew she was asking more than for me to surf. She was asking me to embrace her in a way I hadn't been able to. She wanted me to choose her over my fears and dislike of the ocean. Morgan did it, but I could tell it wasn't enough. She had a longing in her eyes that drew me in and pushed me away at the same time. I thought I loved her more than Morgan, which made me ashamed. The wish for a sister, not a twin.

"Well, you won't be missing much. My dad has a grand plan of getting my mom out of the chair and going for a mini-hike. He pulled out the pictures of her being active, trying to see if we remembered any of the good times. I think it's more important to him than it is to her. Life before the walker. Life before the chair. I try to tell him it's just life. We don't care. It's not like I have deep regret over not earning a Girl Scout camping badge. I don't even like nature. Everyone knows that." Morgan reached us and his board. Brooke flashed him a smile and a hang-ten symbol with her hand.

"He's just trying to connect with you guys. Try to appreciate it." Again, I cringed. I knew. Ungrateful. Her mom was dead. My parents were just annoying. She turned her attention back to Morgan.

"Wasn't sure you would handle that last one. I was sure you would catch cracks." Brooke's language often reminded us of the life she led before she came to California. She thought Morgan would get beaten up by the rocks and waves, and he had a slight cut on his foot.

"Just one. Muri, first aid, please."

Luckily, I felt no pain in my foot. Once again, the twin connection was proven false. I grabbed the kit of antiseptic and Band-Aids that I kept in my things. I did my best school nurse and fixed him up.

"Muri, don't forget, Spencer is meeting us at the house." Brooke laughed as she saw my eyes widen.

"Spencer? I thought you had invited Wes. When did this happen?"

"Ah, get over it. He threw a rock at you when you were in the third grade and he said it was an accident. It was a million years ago. Get over it."

"You should have my back and hold grudges as long as I say the grudge is still valid." Morgan frowned and walked away toward the car, mumbling the whole way. The wind caught a word or two and carried it back to us. I clearly could hear his affection for me. "Mental...." Brooke stopped giggling and looked at me seriously.

"You know Spencer threw that rock at you to get your attention. You know he still likes you."

I shrugged. "I know. But that's not the point. I think Morgan would take anyone's side but mine." She frowned at me.

"I'm not sure I ever know what the point is, Muri. But I love you, Cuz. I love you with all my heart. Try to have some fun." I smiled.

I gave her a big hug, not caring that sand would coat me. It was worth it. In my heart, I thought we were sisters. We packed up our gear, and the three of us crammed into a beat-up PT Cruiser with the surfboards strapped to the top. This was Brooke's ride. Morgan and I were fifteen and had no privileges. Morgan had a skateboard he made work, and I had a vintage-looking yellow Schwinn that I called Butter. She was a smooth ride, and she looked like butter. Not too complex. It got me where I needed to be most days since we were still part of ... carpool. I shuddered at the thought. Thankfully, we were heading into summer, and when we returned to the drudgery of the school year, at least one of us would be a driver.

It was a short ride. We had made it to the beach on our own many times. It was the boards that made it a challenge. As we pulled around that last corner off of Monroe Street onto our street, Murray Hill, Brooke pulled a little too close to the cars parked along the street. Morgan gasped, and we couldn't help but laugh. He was our cautious one, out of the water. He truly was the defender of the rules and the worrier of our clan. My first aid kit was more about practicality versus fear of injury. My laugh ended abruptly when I saw our driveway. There was an enormous RV camper parked halfway in our driveway and halfway in the street.

"Holy crap. He's for real. Did you know he was doing this?" Now it was Morgan's turn to laugh.

"Yeah. Spencer's dad said we could use it. I guess they never take it out, and he knows Mom is sort of limited, you know."

"Oh, okay. I guess it was nice of him. But what did you say about Mom that he felt like being so generous?" I knew Brooke could feel the tension in the car. She set the parking brake quickly, and we were quickly escorted from the Cruiser.

"Check it! Out-n-z da twins. Luv ya, but I'm starved. See you on the other side." I glared at Morgan. He ignored me and thanked Brooke for the ride. She hopped out and helped him with his board. They exchanged a long hug.

"I hope your mom has fun. You did a good thing." I was stung by this show of support for my two-minute-younger sibling. Brooke came over to me and gave me the same hug. I stiffened, and she released me. "Try to have fun, Cuz. Just try." I nodded as my dad joined us outside. Brooke blew him a kiss. "Have fun, Uncle Mitch! I'll be over for a family dinner this week when you guys get back."

My dad Mitch. Mitchell Lutey, artist and professor extraordinaire. He was definitely something...I just wasn't sure what that something was. For as long as I could remember, he had been busy working on his "latest" installation. He got a gig to do some public art bus stop benches, and that was it. When we were little, he worked at the community college teaching art and running the wood shop. He had dabbled in metalwork in his undergraduate school but didn't really focus on it. He fell in love with my mom. They had us, and all was wonderful (or so the story was told)—then came the bus stops and the female undergrad assistants. I think nothing was going on except a constant ego boost. They featured the metalwork benches in a local magazine. He took a good photo with his sandy blond hair, deep blue eyes, and smirk of a smile. He became a bit of a sensation—and was given more classes to teach, eventually tenure, and a metals studio at our house. That was about the time my mom got really sick. She had an autoimmune disorder—or in other words, we don't know exactly what's wrong with you, but it's not good, it's getting worse, and oh yeah—your body is doing it to yourself. Nothing like being your own worst enemy.

"Brooke, I wish you'd reconsider coming with us. Your mom and I used to have so much fun camping when we were your age. So many good times. Muri could use a pal on the trip." Brooke teared up and pivoted to her car.

"Nah—no thanks."

Morgan and I were in my dad's face within seconds. This was definitely a twin thing. "What is wrong with you?" we echoed in unison.

"What? I miss your aunt. It would have been good for us to connect."

"Good for you, Dad. Good for you."

Spencer rolled up with his duffel, and Morgan walked away without another word. I couldn't let it go. "You are so unaware and uninvolved. She's having a hard time." He gave me a stern look with no remorse.

"We all are. She never asks how I feel about things. I lost my sister too." My eyes widened to the point where I thought they burst free from my face.

"I forgot. It's about how it all affects you. I always forget to take that note. Let me jot it down now. How is this really about the very important Mitch Lutey?"

My dad held out his hand.

"You've lost it for the entire weekend. Remember, this is your consequence, not mine. The disrespect is getting out of hand. I understand the whole teen angst thing, but that's enough." I handed him my phone. Now I was truly isolated with this group of people I called my family. They could pack the camper themselves.

"Call me when it's time to go." I sauntered inside the house. I was in no hurry to face my mother, the ever-devoted yet ailing Mrs. Lutey, aka my mom Lorelei. She was a woman of simple style and simple needs. She was also a bit of a mystery. My father could trace his DNA and ancestral lineage back for generations. We heard about it quite a bit. There was even a plaque on the wall that had a funky little poem about our ancestor who lived eons ago. Dad took pride in the mere age of the name. I think it grounded him. But Mom, her story was sad and continuing to be mildly tragic. She was an orphan from somewhere in upstate New York—we had never been there—so that in itself was a mystery. We were West Coast people. We'd never been east of Texas. They shuttled my mother to an orphanage in Pennsylvania, where a family adopted her. They suspected that she had actually been born out of the country— maybe Canada or Scotland. That part was always hazy. Her adoptive parents had long since passed away, so there was no one to ask. They were apparently already ancient when they adopted her. Here she was, looking excited about the trip. I guess that meant I should try to muster some kindness toward the situation. She really didn't have much except us.

"Hey, Mom." She turned, using her walker to help balance. She came in for a warm embrace and kiss.

"My sweetheart. Why so glum?" I shrugged.

"You already packed?" I fixed an errant button on her blouse. She looked deep into my eyes and brushed the hair away from my face. She kissed me softly on the cheek.

"My sweet child. You don't have to worry or take care of me. I'm fine. I will be fine." I could feel the tears building up pressure in my eyes. I willed them away. I took a deep breath and tried to sound sincere.

"I know, Mom." My resolve would last only for a few seconds. "Gonna finish packing." I rushed out of the room. She called out after me.

"Muriel, don't forget the s'mores!" Forgetting the s'mores was the least of my worries. Today was not a good day. In less than an hour I would be traveling with this lot, with no technological escape. Thank God for sketch pads. Apparently, I inherited my parents' gift for art. My parents met at art school. It would only make sense that at least one of their progeny would pursue the same path. My preference is for 2D drawing—no computers, please. I peeked outside, and the hustle and bustle continued. Like a line of ants, Dad, Morgan, and Spencer loaded the RV. I could hear them chattering about being preppers and getting ready for anything out in nature. Spencer seemed to have taken the role of lead survival expert.

"Water—you've got to have water. That's the most important. Without that, we're all dead." I closed the blinds and continued to pack my "go bag": sketch pad, pencils, fine-tip markers, graham crackers, chocolate, and marshmallows. I was ready. They were packed and by the RV. There was a knock on my bedroom door. It was my mother.

"Muri, we're all set." I didn't make her wait. I grabbed my bag and went.

Chapter 2

The interior of the RV was swanky. I always knew that Spencer's family had more cash than we did, but now I really understood the extent. The boys were sitting in a living room area playing video games on a built-in flat screen. I was reclining on a cushy couch. My dad was driving, and my mom was enjoying being the copilot. So far, the ride wasn't miserable at all. In fact, no one had noticed my brooding, and the scenery on the way was beautiful. My mom had always wanted to see the redwoods, and I was glad we were taking her to see the ancient trees. It was about a thirteen-hour drive straight through, but we planned on making a stop in Solvang, California. We'd stay the night nearby. My father was obsessed with the work of Edvard Eriksen and his bronze work Den Lille Havfure (Danish for The Little Mermaid). He had always wanted to see the original, which sits on a rock in Copenhagen, Denmark, but he had never left the country. He hadn't even gone to Mexico with us when we went, which was basically like walking across the street. Solvang was like a little Denmark in California, and they had a copy of the bronze work displayed there. He was fascinated by how such a seemingly benign metal work that depicted the mermaid from Hans Christian Andersen's story The Little Mermaid had become the target of so many vandals and political movements. It had been destroyed and repaired, like, ten times.

My mom looked like she was ready to take a break from sitting straight up as copilot. Her long black hair was coming loose from her tight bun. She said it was easier to not have to think about her hair. She got up carefully from the front seat to take a break in the back with us. Morgan hopped up immediately and acted as her crutch, but she seemed okay. I was pretty surprised by it. Other than looking a little tired, she looked good. I moved over so she could have the best spot on the RV couch.

"How are you holding up, Muriel? Is the video game noise getting to you yet?" She stroked my hair. She had a gentle way of petting me, as if I were really some wild beast she was soothing. Apparently I had been a screamer as a young child.

"It's fine. It's been a fairly smooth ride back here."

"I bet you already miss Brooke."

"Speaking of Brooke, did you hear the horrible thing that Dad said to her?"

"Yes. I'm not sure it was horrible though. You know the loss of his sister has been intense for him, too. It was just the two of them—like you and Morgan."

"I guess."

She looked out the window. The sun was setting, and the ocean was in clear view.

"This is the view we should have every day," my mom muttered.

Just then my dad pulled off of the highway, taking the exit toward the Soaring Sails RV resort. This was the place for travelers like myself who preferred glamping, except most of the clientele was of legal boozy age. We were in the heart of the Santa Ynez Valley and their wine country, sort of near Santa Barbara. As we drove through the resort, we passed souped-up Airstreams, cottages, and safari-style tents. There was a place for a communal bonfire and a fairly nice pool. But I didn't notice any children or teens around.

The little cottages positioned near the RV hookups were all designed with small white picket fences surrounding a cozy porch. Glampers occupied each porch, sipping glasses of wine and watching the sunset. I thought this was why my dad had picked this location. My mother never drank. I don't know if she ever had, but now, her body wouldn't tolerate medication and alcohol. Lately, I had seen my dad making it part of his regular nightly routine. My dad's phone chimed with a text. He read it and chuckled. The cliché of the admiring female undergrad. He was a good guy, but he thrived on the adoration and ego boost. His only in-house fan was my mother. She acted as if she were under his spell. No matter what I heard her say or how I saw her feeling and reacting, she always supported his will. Maybe she felt dependent or guilty about being sick—God only knew. I loved him, but I saw right through him. So did Morgan. Dad pulled the RV into its spot.

"Did you guys see the pool? Why don't you go for a swim?" Morgan and Spencer were still playing their video game. Morgan didn't even glance in my dad's direction.

"Trying to get rid of us already, Mitch?"

My mom piped in. "Come on, guys. You know we don't like you calling your father by his first name. It's very disrespectful." Spencer looked uncomfortable. Morgan put the game controller down.

"Okay, Mom. So are you already trying to get rid of us, Dad?" Mitch pulled out a bottle of wine from one of the RV cabinets. I could call him Mitch all I wanted in my head. As I thought this, Morgan looked at me and gave me an odd smirk. I felt sort of caught in the thought. Sometimes I thought he knew what I was thinking.

"Yes, I think I'd like to sit out here and watch the sunset with your mom. This is our vacation, too." He helped my mom up and they walked outside. He set some chairs up and brought out a blanket for her. Okay, he loved her, but in the hierarchy of love—he came first.

I put my sketch book down and remarked, "It smells like rain. I'm just going to stay in here." It didn't rain. The boys swam. My parents drank wine. I fell asleep and had an odd dream that had plagued me off and on my whole life. I hadn't had it in years, but I remembered it always as the same weird dream—like an old annoying relative that you don't recognize until they pinch your cheeks.

The Dream: I was alone, I was at the edge of the ocean, and there were creepy clams or oysters or something biting my feet. This time Spencer made an appearance and helped pry one loose that was attached to my big toe. I found his appearance in my dream to be the most disturbing element of all. I forced myself to wake up. I looked around and everyone was back inside the RV. The boys had resumed video gaming without the volume. My mom was tucked into bed. My dad was finishing the bottle of wine in the captain's chair. We'd all found our spots for the night. I looked at Spencer more closely. Would he help me if oysters were stuck to my toes? Spencer—when we were young, before the rock incident—was my friend. We were all part of the same after-school-your-parents-can't-pick-you-up-and-you're-too-young-to-go-home programs. He was quiet and kind and liked to color with me when everyone else wanted to make their fingers into guns and everything else into a weapon.

Then things changed. All of his parents' hard work paid off and his latchkey existence was no more. He got to go home after school, and someone was there waiting for him. I'd see him around the school, at the beach, or in town, but we weren't close anymore. The situation that had brought us together had ended—by his choice or not, he deserted me. I tried to forget that I had even had him as a friend. It was easier to pretend we never had been friends. I guess he didn't like that, and hence the rock. I needed one painful stitch—that was enough to cement my hatred for him. Except everyone knew, including him, that it wasn't true. I didn't hate him. I couldn't. It was just that he was my only friend other than Morgan. I didn't know how I could feel so lonely as a child but never actually be alone. Twins are never alone. They don't even exist in someone's mind without the other one.

Spencer had shed all his awkwardness and was arguably the most handsome boy in our class, next to Morgan. He maintained the casual beach look. His hair was always two weeks past clean cut. On most days, sunglasses covered his hazel eyes and long eyelashes. Spencer was a natural athlete, clever, and still kind. If there was a vote for anything, someone would write his name down for "most" something. I had turned out to be "least" something. Least likely to be friends with Spencer again, for certain. Or maybe there was hope?

Day two: On to Solvang. We left the RV park early because Solvang was just a stop on the way. It was the redwoods—those ancient trees—that we were taking my mother to see. She was a print maker when she met my dad. She focused on the avian world, inspired by the old Audubon books of birds she would see in the library. She sat out the cold Pennsylvania winters cuddled up to an art book, studying the work of her idols like Edward Lear or John Gould. Nature and its many shades fascinated her. She once told me she believed there were at least a hundred subtle shades of green. These trees had always captivated her. She thought they had an ancient wisdom. I think somehow she thought connecting with nature could give her the answers to who she was. If she was part of nature, then it didn't matter where she came from or who her family was. She could just exist with meaning, without the knowledge of a beginning. As her body rebelled and attacked itself and her autoimmune system broke the rules of how it should care for her, she abandoned nature. But as we got farther away from the house and deeper on this trip to the forest, she seemed to be returning to us. I didn't think nature had abandoned her.

The hungry teenage boys mandated our first stop in Solvang. The entire town looked like they plucked it from a fairytale—windmills and Danish-designed buildings. Intricate wooden details adorned the windows and doors of the structures. We parked the RV in a lot for tourists and made our way on foot through the quaint town. We'd all done our research on what we wanted to see. We brought my mother's scooter so she could experience everything the way we were. We landed at a tiny little café where the menu listed hearty breakfasts of eggs and bacon, but their specialty was aebleskiver. Aebleskiver are basically the most delicious doughnuts, though some think they are more like pancake balls. We ate ours with a red mixed-berry jam. I caught myself stealing glances at Spencer. Morgan caught me, too. He shook his head in disapproval. He didn't know what I was thinking. Not even I knew what I was thinking. I was just looking. I was looking and remembering. Then out of nowhere Spencer spoke—to me.

"So Muri, what are you hoping to sketch out there? Is your perspective going to be on the ground looking up at those giants? Or do you have something else in mind?" He didn't glance up from his fork filled with aebleskiver and jam. He just took another bite. My hands were suddenly cold and clammy. Had he seen me looking at him, too? How dare he talk to me like old friends—well, at least without warning me we still counted as old friends? He hadn't said two words to me on the drive so far. This was an alarming break of grudge etiquette and established social norms. Was he allowed to sweep it under the rug? I didn't know. I secretly hoped so. My processing halted as he looked up from his plate while taking a neatly organized bite. He was waiting for my response. Everyone was.

"I, uh, I don't know."

"Well, I'll be interested to see what you come up with. You always had such a great eye for those types of details." Bloody hell! I was breaking out my TV British now. Was this allowed? Did he freaking compliment me? Did that just happen? As I sat stunned, a strong pinch brought me back to the present. It was my mother, under the table. She pinched my thigh and bought me some time.

"Yes, I've always thought Muriel had an interesting perspective with angles and shadow. She really hasn't spent too much time in this type of nature before. Mainly, she's seen the flat open areas, plains, valleys, and the beach views. These towering trees will be a challenge for sure." She patted my leg, prompting me to respond.

"Yes, I'll figure it out when I get there. Excuse me, everyone. Ladies' room." I fled to the bathroom, then waited outside for everyone. I wasn't returning to that table or that scene. I noticed our café sat catty-corner to the reason my father was here. The statue. The greening patina on The Little Mermaid was flaky and distracting. I found nothing appealing about her. So it was easy for the historical plaques and other information that surrounded her, which included a blurb about Hans Christian Andersen, his museum, and his paper-cutting skills, to distract me. I had never heard of this before. He folded paper and cut it while telling stories. The folded paper cuttings became intricate designs and scenes from the stories he was telling.

Morgan and Spencer were the first ones to emerge from the café. Morgan waved from across the street.

"We're off to get Viking hats and wooden shoes!"

My mom walked out of the café toward her scooter. My father was two paces behind her. He and I exchanged a hopeful glance. She was walking on her own without a cane or my father's arm. We both smiled like all was right with the world. I motioned and pointed to the statue. They crossed to meet me. The boys strolled down the street far too loudly for morning—or any day of the week. I was glad to have some physical distance from them. My father gazed at the statue with disappointment. He got in close and looked at it from all sides. "Maybe it's the placement. I'm not impressed."

"Well, it is a reproduction and doesn't possess any of the historical significance that appealed to you," my mom suggested.

"That's true. Anderson's Little Mermaid story is tragic, and the namesake statue seems to emulate it." My dad leaned in to touch it. "Except it perseveres. It's repaired, moved, refinished, and given a new life after each vandal or storm. I wish we could all be renewed in such a way."

My mother sighed as she analyzed the piece of art. I put my arm around her.

"You seem like you're doing better here. How are you feeling?" She thought about it and smiled, then looked off in the distance as if she was visiting some far-off thought.

"I do feel better. Maybe it's just getting out and a change of scenery."

"Dad, I want to go check out the Hans Christian Andersen Museum. Wanna go? They have some of his paper-cutting artwork there." I could tell it pleased my dad that the thaw was on. Maybe our icy relationship had some hope. There was hope only when we saw hope for my mother. Our relationships were all so intricately woven and undeniably fragile.

"So why did you say The Little Mermaid was tragic? It's lighthearted."

My dad put his arm around me. The three of us headed toward Morgan and Spencer, who were gliding in and out of shops, trying to find the perfect Viking helmet. "In the original story she dies. She doesn't get the prince," my dad said bluntly.

My mom shuddered. "She's actually tortured in the story. At one point, painful oysters attach to her tail. I imagine that would be like the nerve pain I feel in my legs." My dad squeezed my mom's hand and kissed her on the cheek. I too would have wanted to reach out to my mother and transmit some of my strength to her. (I often felt as if I could do this, even though I knew it was wishful thinking.) Yet I couldn't think of anything but the oysters attaching to her tail. Did my parents tell me this version of the story when I was a child? Did they traumatize me by stealing my beautiful version of Disney's mermaid? Was this why I was plagued by this dream? I knew they had revealed Santa, the Easter Bunny, and the Tooth Fairy, but had they also waged war on Disney princesses, and I had blocked it out? At least that would explain that dream.

Morgan's shopping adventure was complete. He had a Viking helmet (which he was wearing), wooden clogs (which he was also wearing), and a Danish stein that he had poured his water bottle into. He would have looked silly if Spencer hadn't trumped his look by adding a fake two-handed sword. Morgan took a swig from his stein.

"Where to? I think we're done." Spencer and Morgan clinked steins and toasted Solvang. "To Solvang, this weird little Danish town." My mom took a picture of the boys and giggled. "We're off to the Hans Christian Andersen museum." Morgan looked like he approved. Spencer seemed genuinely interested. "Did you know he wrote *Thumbelina* and *The Ugly Duckling*?" my mom asked while taking more photos of the boys.

"No, but I think I need one of those swords. We'll meet you guys there." Morgan sprinted back to the shops again, and Spencer kept up. He called back, "Also more aebleskivers!" My dad was giving the Mermaid one last look before we headed toward the museum. He shook his head.

"I really thought it would be more impressive."

My mom looped her hand through his and kissed him on the cheek. "Sorry, sweetheart. Maybe we can see the real thing in Denmark someday?"

We got to the entrance of the museum and a sign on the front door said "Closed for renovations." A small blond senior citizen walked by us as I tried to peek in through the windows.

"It's closed for renovations, sweetie."

My dad stood close and peeked through the window, too.

"Sorry, Muri."

The woman continued her hospitality. "If you're looking for something to do with your family, we have our beautiful Nojoqui Falls nearby. It's quite beautiful, about 80 feet tall, I believe. If you take Alisal Road, you'll be right there. There's hiking and picnicking. It's a lot of fun." My mom's eyes lit up as she heard this. She looked at me and raised her eyebrows. I knew she wanted to go.

"What do you think, Muriel? Should we try it? I'd love to see the falls." My father tried to add to the coaxing. I was sorry they thought I'd be such a hard sell. "I'm sure you'd find something to sketch there."

I shrugged, slightly annoyed that I was being treated like some child who would have a tantrum because the museum was closed. I guess I might have been acting like that lately. Was I really so difficult?

"Sure. Sounds like fun." My parents breathed a sigh of relief. Which annoyed me.

Two loud Vikings with two-handed swords returned. "So what's up?" Morgan showed off his new sword. "You like?" I frowned at his sword play. He then showed me his bounty of aebleskivers.

"The museum is closed. We're going to check out some falls that are nearby." The boys stuffed the aebleskivers in their mouths. Morgan offered one up to me.

"Thanks." He grinned and reached into his bag. "I also got you something else." He placed a Viking helmet on my head. "Now it's a vacation!"

My mom hurried to get her camera before I took it off. I had no intention of taking it off. I wanted to be a good sport, no matter what. I wished I didn't hate the helmet, though. It was making my head sweaty, but I wasn't taking it off. It smelled weird, like off-gassing of VOCs or something. I was sure it was made of some weird plastic from China. Why didn't he get me the clogs? At least those were made of wood. I was smiling, though—smiling. Happy. Happy thoughts. My mother took at least fifty photos. She even made us pose again in front of The Little Mermaid with my dad. We were the stuff of scrapbook legends. We all piled happily into the RV, leaving this tiny bit of Denmark behind and possibly taking with us the beginning of a family rebirth.

Chapter 3

It really was a very short drive to the mildly difficult to pronounce Nojoqui (Naw-ho-wee) Falls—the 164-foot falls named after a former Native American Chumash village nearby. The falls were close in height to Niagara Falls. I knew these things because Morgan had been reading statistics and the history of the place from a pamphlet he grabbed on our way out of town. It said that this was the rainiest part of the region. The natural spring and falls flowed all year because of the heavy rainfall. The sky had been threatening to rain for days, but this was Southern California—we didn't believe the clouds or the weather forecast. We found a great place to park, close to the amazing scenery. It emboldened my mother to go on a short walk with my father, with only a walking stick. Morgan and Spencer took off in search of adventure and maybe a swim in the falls. They graciously invited me to join them, but this view really was breathtaking. My mother was right. There would be something to sketch here. I grabbed my little go bag of art tools and ventured off to find a good view of the falls where I wouldn't get any spray. My supplies and I would stay safe and dry. I found just the spot near a large rock: high enough to see, and far enough away to stay dry. Even though the falls were very high, they were surprisingly thin: three or four almost wisps of water pouring down in front of a massive rock face and then barely hiding a little cave at the bottom behind the falls. More of a nook than a cave. I saw Morgan and Spencer coming around the side, considering whether to take a dip in the pool of water at the base of the falls. I scrunched behind a tree branch, hoping not to be seen. This was my spot, and I wasn't ready to give it up. Spencer looked closely at the water.

"It's murky."

Morgan took a closer look.

"I concur—no parasites in my brain today, thank you. I'd like to go home amoeba-free!"

They took a few pictures of themselves in front of the falls and kept moving along the trail. That's when the rain started. It sprinkled at first. Then suddenly it was a rainstorm, a complete downpour. Morgan and Spencer ran off into the meadow toward the RV. I quickly tried to grab my supplies and shove them into my bag. The moss on the rock didn't provide a lot of traction. I was slipping. I slid off one side of the rock, and my supplies went down the other. They were just paper and pens, but the sketches—the sketches would be lost forever! I trudged through what was becoming a bog-like mud path to the other side of the rock to collect my things.

The rain was joined by intense wind and was now falling sideways. My mud bog path turned into a stream of uprooted plants and sticks floating past me. My sketchbook was dirty and soaked but back in my possession and safely tucked in my waterproof bag. I convinced myself that it was not wet all the way through and that it would dry and be fine. The wind picked up a stick and smacked it into my face, scratching me. I was suddenly alert and aware the waterfall was no longer a wisp. The sound of the water crashing down over the rock was deafening. The previously tranquil pool was flooding. Then I heard it. I heard it over the crashing of the water and the whistling of the wind—it was a cry. Or more of a shriek. Something, some animal, sounded injured.

My first instinct was to run as far away from the shriek as I could—to use all of my strength and pry my feet free from the muddy earth and make my way back to the RV. But then I heard it again, and I couldn't move. The shriek sounded more like words. Those seconds of non-movement made a difference. My hesitation killed my chance to break free from the muddy trap. I was no longer on the sideline away from the falls. I was already halfway engulfed by the swelling pool and the flash flood traveling down the meadow. The shriek again—this time audible as language—had paralyzed me.

"Help me!" The voice was closer to the falls than to the rock I was escaping. I splashed around, trying to get my bearings. "Help me!" Something drew me closer to the cascade. My feet were no longer in mud. I was swimming. I spied the dry cave under the waterfall. My bag on my back, I did my best freestyle and reached the base of the torrent. The water crashed down with such force that it pushed me backwards. The water got in my eyes, ears, nose, but I kept my mouth closed, saving my breath. I knew that I had to dive under the falls to make it to the dry cave, which was slightly higher than the pool. Water was creeping in, but it seemed to have an outlet somewhere, so it drained quickly.

"Help me!" I could still hear it. I seemed to be closer now. But my mind kicked into pure survival mode. I wasn't looking to reach the voice. I was trying to stay alive. The pounding of my heart in my ears blocked out whatever voice was calling out. I dove down, careful to feel my way for sharp rocks and obstacles to my safe landing ahead. I reached the slimy rock on the other side of the falls and attempted to pull my heavy body to safety. My drenched clothes weighed more than my arms could seem to bear. I tried to find a footing to help me into the cave and out of the water. I made one last effort and slid up into the damp cave out of the storm. I took a deep breath and said quiet prayers of thanks. The storm couldn't last much longer. This was California, I tried to remind myself. We were in a drought. It took me a moment to realize that I was not alone in the cave. I focused on my breath, trying to remain calm. I imagined my best inner yogi, but I was shivering, and my breath was shallow. I didn't want to look. I heard the click, click of little claw-like movements getting closer to me. Then a sweet voice, melodic, the same one I heard as a shriek before whispered, very close to me. So close I could feel the hot breath on my neck.

"Did you come to help me? I don't think so."

My shivering stopped as the fear paralyzed me. I took a deep breath and tried to see by moving no part of me other than my eyes. And I could see. It was a smallish creature with the half body of a bird, talons and wing-like arms leading up to the torso of a mini human. Its face looked dry and wrinkled, with cracking split skin near its mouth. Its feathers were wet and tattered, but I could still see the brilliant blues and purples of its plumage. The skin on the arms, tinged with colors of the rainbow, but very light and subtle, looked silky. Its hair was a combination of feathers woven into silky strands of green. I screamed. I may have mentioned before that my mother treated me like a wild animal that she was trying to soothe. As a child I was prone to outbursts, fits, and tantrums. To say now that I screamed might have been an understatement. I jumped up, flailed my arms around, made my hands into fists, tried to swing with purpose—screamed and screamed and jumped into the falls. I'm sure my fists landed on some part of the creature's body. I vaguely remembered a terrified look on the beast's face.

This was the last thing that I remembered concretely. The rest was like a dream. I could see Morgan—he was wading into the water. The rain had stopped. There was a body face down in what was now a river. He spotted the figure and rushed toward it. I now recognized my bag, which was still on my back. I was floating face down. As he got close to me, he noticed the shimmering scales of some sort of fish. It nudged at my torso. Morgan was almost to me, and he realized there were dozens of silvery fish circling me and nudging gently at my skin. He thought they were nibbling my flesh, trying to eat me. He believed he was in a full-on piranha moment. So here we establish that both of the Lutey twins are highly successful at freaking out with an extreme level of intensity. He flipped me over and began his best ninja impression. He karate chopped fish, kicked, and shouted at them.

"Get the hell off my sister!" The fish scattered. He saw Spencer rushing into the water to help. They dragged me to dryer land, and Spencer began mouth-to-mouth, starting compressions and humming "Staying Alive" by the Bee Gees to keep the beat of the thrusts. (He's lifeguard-trained.) Morgan made the sign of the cross and tried to remember any childhood prayer that he could. It had been a while since we'd been to church. Then that was it. I spit out water, coughed, and my eyes opened. Morgan grabbed me and held me close. His tears ran down my face. I was dazed but hugged him back. I remembered the creature and felt panicked again.

"Did you see it? The creature?"

He nodded.

"Yes, I did. It was a weird fish and then there were all these other fish that were trying to get at you." I scrunched my face up, confused.

"Fish?" The boys helped me to my feet, but I was wobbly. Morgan picked me up and carried me out of the meadow. My parents were waiting by the RV. My mother rushed to me with amazing ease, as if she'd never felt a moment of pain.

"What happened?"

"We found her in the water." Morgan started to tell my mom about the events, but Spencer put a hand on his shoulder to quiet him. Morgan left the part out about the flesh-eating fish.

"She's okay, though. I think. You're okay—right, Muri?" I nodded.

"How long was I in the water?" He recapped the timeline. I guess I hadn't been for very long. Morgan was looking for me, and Spencer heard my screams. He joked about recognizing a classic Muriel meltdown.

"It reminded me of the good ol' days of kid time after school." Morgan and I both glared at him. He smiled sheepishly. Inside the

RV, my mom put a blanket around me. My dad looked in my eyes and took my pulse.

"You guys, I think this trip is over. I want to get your sister home. I'll call Dr. Thompson and see if we should bring her in to get looked at." Everyone was fine about heading back, except me.

"Mom, I'm so sorry. I don't want to ruin the trip." My mom kissed my forehead. "It's been wonderful already. It's been just perfect."

Morgan chimed in.

"Sure, if you don't count me finding my sister face down in water being eaten by fish!"

My mother looked shocked. "What?"

Spencer shook his head. "She's okay. I was encouraging you to edit that."

My dad started up the RV. "We're going to get you checked out at the nearest urgent care. Somebody please find one between here and home." The closest medical facility was in Santa Barbara, the opposite way. Dad wanted us to head north and get me checked. My mother seemed uncomfortable about stopping in Santa Barbara.

"Mitch, why don't we just head back down the coast. I'd rather have Muriel seen closer to home. What if they decide to admit her—I think it will be too…."

I chimed in. "Yeah, Dad, I'm good. I can definitely wait until we're in San Diego." I looked at Morgan. His face had gone white. I suddenly realized the significance of Santa Barbara. Everyone remembered this was where Aunt Mallory had been lost at sea. Dad visited every hospital, urgent care, and halfway house for weeks, hoping his sister would turn up. They never recovered her body. Morgan put his hand on my dad's shoulder.

"I was exaggerating, Dad. She's okay. She'll be okay. Let's just go home."

Mitchell Lutey, in this moment, was more fragile than I had ever seen him. Maybe he cared more than I thought. He started to cry, and

I hugged this man that sometimes seemed like such a stranger. He was so different from me—or maybe we were more alike than I would have liked to believe. He squeezed me tight.

"I never want to lose you or anyone else in this family."

Spencer was awkwardly hanging back in the RV. We made our best attempt at a group hug. My mom tucked me into a spot on the couch, and she and my father took the lead—captain and copilot on the road home. I could tell that memories of my aunt had invaded all of our hearts. My mind still buzzed with thoughts of the strange creature by the falls but tried to dismiss it as some head injury delusion. At least I was here safe with my family. Poor Brooke. Two parents go out on a boat and only one returns. Someone might have suspected foul play, but my uncle, Nohea Kainoa, washed up on shore and spent a week in the hospital recovering. They had been on a romantic anniversary trip. They didn't live here yet. Who leaves Hawaii for romance in California? They met in Hawaii when my Aunt Mallory was starting her first job after college as part of a research team. She did her college thesis on the lifespan of coral and how the environment was changing their life expectancy. The waters in Hawaii were getting warmer, and they were having a bleaching event (basically killing coral). Her team's job was to put a time-lapse camera underwater and document the coral changes based on the temperature. My uncle was also a researcher, already studying the weather changes in the islands. They both cared passionately about how it was changing the landscape of his homeland above and below the water—which led to lots of collaboration, and eventually Brooke.

Well, they had been visiting San Diego for a few days and left Brooke with us while they went on a Santa Barbara excursion. They boarded a 41-foot yacht with thirteen other passengers on a private whale-watching dinner cruise. The entire vessel was lost. All the crew and passengers, other than Mallory, survived. My aunt and uncle had been on this trip before when Brooke was a small baby. In the fall, Pacific gray whales made their way down the coast south to the warm waters of Baja, California. This southern migration was what they observed on the first trip that they took. They had always wanted to see the return trek of the whales heading back north in the spring with their calves, traveling the coast to Alaska. Uncle Nohea said that Mallory and the rest of the passengers were marveling over their supreme luck. They not only got to see the gray whales, but humpback and blue whales too. It was very rare to see these majestic creatures in one area at the same time. He said it was like an aquatic traffic jam. The water was clearer than usual; he said it seemed shallow—like they could see all the way to the bottom.

The whales appeared to angle for a spot to look at the passengers on the boat. First the whales surrounded the yacht, spaced out far enough not to create extra motion on deck. Then they started to breach. They leaped and whirled, almost in unison. Everyone aboard the boat was in awe—cameras flashed, and they cheered as each new whale seemed to perform for them. Then the passengers noticed the motion. The boat swayed high and unevenly. The crew cautioned everyone to get back from the sides and grab a nearby life vest, just in case things got even rockier. As people scrambled, suddenly the whales leaped and submerged. The boat was still, once again. The passengers caught their breath. My uncle said that he embraced my aunt. He said that they were relieved, grateful, and so in love. It was that last moment that haunted him.

The man next to him was the first to notice the spyhopping. (This is when a whale pops just their head out of the water to look.) One whale after another surrounded the boat, popping its head out of the water and looking at its contents—terrified tourists emitting shrieks and cries. Nohea held my aunt tightly and whispered in her ear: "It'll be all right. We're safe here. They're just taking a glance at us, for a change." My aunt relaxed and smiled. Then they both saw it. A blue whale surfaced with another creature. He believed the creature wasn't a whale or dolphin. It was something with a shiny, glittering tail of gold and green. It dove and splashed, then seemed to rest on the body of the enormous whale, with its back facing the boat. He didn't see if it was a male or female. Its back was covered by fur or hair or scales—he couldn't tell—it just glittered as the sun was setting on the sea. He knew this was no regular sea creature. It raised an arm and gave a signal to the whales. An arm! After that, the boat swayed and capsized. He woke up in the hospital two days later. In Hawaii, he had heard the tales of water deities. Now he was a believer, convinced it was a sea spirit or maybe even the water goddess Namaka herself.

A sea spirit and his sister's demise—it was too much for my father. Raised in the Lutheran faith (what I like to call "Catholic Lite"), it mortified him that the story's retelling included this detail. My father barely went to church, but his faith ran deep—like DNA deep. They were religious pillars of the community and definitely part of the group of people who would have been hunting you during the Salem witch trials. They were cross-wearing, holy-water-loving, curse-breaking townspeople. The two family names they carried were the Luteys and the Pellars. The Pellars got rid of all kinds of evil, ungodly influence, and the Luteys were healers. Maybe that's why my dad was always trying to fix my mother.

My opinion at the time was that Uncle Nohea had lost his mind. He was in the middle of a super-stressful situation and had seen a seal or some other whale. Also, it was a freak event. One time I asked Brooke what she thought of the whole story. "I believe that he believes it. I'm not taking anything else from him." Now I, too, had an "experience" with a creature. Who was I going to tell? What did I really see or hear? It talked to me, right? Or maybe I was just hallucinating—maybe I was already floating face down in the river and that was a dream. Yes, I thought, that's what made the most sense. Our brains try to make order out of the chaos, sometimes in strange, fantastical ways. Yet on some level I felt that it was real.

Chapter 4

The RV was no longer in our lives, but Spencer seemed here to stay. He had been at the house almost every day since our return. I was definitely starting to like the idea of him being around, although we weren't really interacting—he was spending all his time with Morgan. They partnered on their science project for the upcoming school science fair. Brooke and I also partnered—just easier to do half of the work with someone you trust. Spencer and Brooke arrived at the house at the same time. It was no coincidence that they arrived at dinnertime. My mother seemed to be in some kind of remission, if that can even happen with autoimmune disease. I guess her body had calmed down and stopped attacking itself for a few days. She was back to her old Betty Crocker ways: cooking. She could make anything. Of all of her gifts, this may have been my most treasured that I missed.

Before her disease, she was the queen of comfort food. And since I was still on the mend, she was pulling out all the stops. Tonight it was beef stroganoff, and chocolate cake covered with fresh strawberries and homemade whipped cream. It seemed like my mother had a secret cookbook related to childhood traumas. The first time she made this dish, I was six. I had begged my mother to sign me up for ballet lessons like the other girls in my first- grade class, but when I arrived, I couldn't go in. I just couldn't do it. It was like there was a force field blocking the door to the studio. No matter how much I wanted to be part of it, be like them and sway to the music—I couldn't do it. I clung to my mother's skirt and cried. Poor Morgan, who had to take the class with me, stood there awkwardly as I cried and my mother tried to pry me from her legs. This was the beginning of my mother charting a course of mother and daughter coping. She would walk to the front desk of whatever we had signed up for (with me attached to her legs, arm, skirt, whatever) and would calmly ask for a refund. Then we would go home, and she would make the most delicious meal ever. I think it healed all three of us. No non-participation scars. It just was.

My dad had even been around more lately. I suspected that he wasn't as heartless as I thought. He might have been staying away because he couldn't help my mother. She was vanishing right before his eyes, so instead of focusing on her fading image, he just looked away. He found solace in his work, in his students, but not in his family. I'm not sure I could understand or forgive that part, but I was trying.

Tonight was special. We were all home for dinner. My dad was sitting at the head of the table, and tonight he skipped his glass of wine. He was just happy to be sitting as lord over his tiny little kingdom of happy people. That is, until my Uncle Nohea arrived. Brooke had forgotten her notebook, and he brought it by just about the time dessert was being served, and he wasn't alone. My uncle worked for NOAA (the National Oceanic and Atmospheric Administration) and often had his own set of interns and grad students trailing him. Tonight it was Colin Irving, a very thin and tall twenty-something with very dark short hair, super-green eyes, and thick glasses. Colin was on loan from Edinburgh University (Scotland) and the Meteorology and Atmospheric Science department. My mother invited them to stay for dessert. My father seemed civil, but he was having trouble hiding his angry tell, which was a subtle, intense flaring of his nostrils followed by a deep breath. Colin was sitting across from Brooke, and I could see she was definitely sending out a vibe. I wasn't sure if it was being received from Colin, but I could have sworn I heard Morgan whispering in my ear that he noticed it too. I looked around—Morgan was still at the other end of the table near Spencer.

Uncle Nohea was the first one to speak. "This is the most delicious chocolate cake, Lorelei. Thank you so much for asking us to stay."

My mother sliced another piece of cake and offered it to Colin, who had gobbled up the first piece as if he hadn't eaten a home-cooked meal—ever. "It's been too long, Nohea. We have missed you." My father directed the conversation to Colin.

"So what are you researching here?" Colin had a rather large bite of cake in his mouth that he tried to wash down quickly so he could answer.

I heard Morgan in my ear again. "Can you believe this guy? What a weirdo." I whipped my head around again. Morgan hadn't moved.

My dad asked, "You okay, Muri?"

"Uh, yeah. I just thought I heard something." This was just enough time for Colin to swallow and answer my father's question.

"Rainbows. I study rainbows formed by sea spray." At this point it seemed like Brooke was going to swoon. This kid had gotten her with ocean rainbows.

"Wow, I've seen those when I'm surfing. They're amazing." Spencer joined the conversation. "Leprechauns on surfboards. I'd like to see that."

I saw that his handsomeness had evolved with time, but his sense of humor had not. It embarrassed me for him and charmed me (pun intended) at the same time. Amazingly, this was the ice breaker that my father and uncle needed. They both laughed and shook their heads. My dad chimed in, saving Spencer.

"And where's the pot of gold? Sunken treasure?" Colin didn't seem amused. He pursed his lips and looked down at his plate.

"This isn't stuff of folklore. Until you really look at the refracted light of a sea spray rainbow, you can't understand the significance of my research." I could hear Morgan in my ear again.

"Wow, settle down, buddy. Just a little rainbow chatter. No one's trying to blow you up." I looked directly at Morgan and tried to speak to him with my eyes, but thought these words:

"Are you talking to me, Morgan? Did you tell that guy to settle down?" Morgan's eyes widened. He looked a little sick and confused as he stared at me. Were we talking to each other? I wondered. Spencer got up and motioned to Morgan.

"Thanks, Mrs. Lutey. The dinner was great, but we've got to make some progress on this science project." Morgan got up silently. I heard nothing else from him until he spoke aloud.

"Nice dinner, guys, thanks—it was great meeting you, Colin. Catch ya later, Unc." My uncle finished his last bite of cake.

"I'm sure you girls have to get to your project. Can I help you clear the table, Lorelei?" My mother was picking up dishes and was looking a little winded.

"Yes, that would we great. I may have overdone it a bit." Both my father and uncle got up to help clear the table before anyone else offered any help. My dad walked over to Nohea and held out his hand to shake it. My uncle put a plate down and embraced him. They both gave in to the deep cleansing hug. As they released from the hug, my uncle wiped his eyes and they said nothing. Each one picked up some dishes and carried them to the kitchen. Then Brooke and my mom shared a knowing glance of relief. Finally, we could move forward. My mom and the men retreated to the kitchen. Colin was keenly aware of the moment.

"You know, I've seen one before."

Brooke bit. "One what?"

"A mermaid."

What the what? Did this guy just blurt that out? We just brokered the freaking peace accord via chocolate cake and he says mermaid? I was trying not to lose my mind. No one ever said mermaid. My uncle said sea creature. Non-whale, non-dolphin, sea creature. Yes, maybe he said sea spirit at one point, but seriously! Thankfully, the only ones within earshot were me and Brooke.

"Hey, buddy. I don't know what you're trying to do, but keep that on lockdown. We don't need any new drama around here."

Brooke looked awakened by the subject.

"Why did you say that? Is that what my dad thought he saw?"

Colin responded with unwavering confidence. "I know that's what he saw. It's another special area of interest of mine."

I stood up and grabbed Brooke's folder.

"Testing local ocean acidity for the science fair isn't going to happen on its own. Busy busy. Nice to meet you, Colin." I tugged at Brooke. My uncle joined us in the dining room.

"Okay, Colin, let's get going." Brooke grabbed her notebook from me.

"You know, Dad, I would like to visit more with you guys back home. So I'll head out, too." Her dad looked puzzled.

"Um, Colin just shared some information with me I'd like to discuss. I feel a bit blown out." Nohea shrugged his shoulders.

"Okay, sweetie." Colin stood up, looking pleased with himself. I was stunned when he looked straight through me and smiled. My parents emerged from the kitchen. He addressed them.

"Thank you for the dessert. I hope to see you lovely folks again soon." My dad stood with his arm around my mother. They both responded happily. "Yes, please come by anytime."

My mom chuckled. "We serve dinner nightly, seven days a week. We remember the college days. You're always welcome, and let me send home some cake with you,"

I chimed in. "I'm sure he has better things to do with his time, Mom."

My parents gave me that "you're rude" look.

"Well, see ya. I hope we don't fail Brooke."

Brooke ignored me. My mom placed a slice of cake on a plate and covered it for him. When he took the cake plate, he put his hand over my mother's hand. My father was busy saying a proper good night to Nohea. Colin spoke quietly to my mother, but I could hear him.

"I'm glad to see you looking so well, Lorelei." My mom, unfazed by his familiarity, smiled an odd question mark of a smile. "Thank you. Have a nice night." The trio left.

"Mom, what was that about?" My mother shrugged.

"Maybe it's Scottish for nice to see you or thanks for having me over."

I wasn't convinced. Colin gave me the creeps and was definitely going on my watch list. I was rarely wrong in the bad vibe department.

Morgan and Spencer had their backpacks on and skateboards.

"Where are you guys going?" my dad asked the boys.

"The beach. We need sand for our project."

"Well, I need sea water for mine—so can I tag along?" I asked.

Spencer smiled. "Got a skateboard?"

"No, I'll just ride Butter." I blushed, realizing this is the first time Spencer had heard me use my bike's name.

Morgan responded for me. "That's what she calls her bike."

Spencer smiled. "All right. That's cool."

My mom handed us some water canteens. (She didn't believe in plastic.) "Be back by dark."

We all nodded yes and headed toward the beach. The late afternoon breeze smelled faintly like the ocean. The sun hung low in the clear sky—not quite ready to set but letting us know that it was on the agenda. It took about fifteen minutes to get to the beach from our house. Our entry point was not where they surfed. The closest spot from our house was a rocky bluff with tide pools at the bottom and a little cove. There was a little private patch of sand, but it spent most of the time getting splashed by the uneven waves crashing against the rocks, so no one went as far as the sand. We stayed on the rocks and explored the tidal pools. When Morgan and I were younger, we considered this our private spot. We'd collect starfish and little crabs, and hunt for sea glass. I didn't mind the slippery rocks or salty sea spray here. It was really just the sand that I minded so much. My dad suspected I had an undiagnosed sensory processing disorder. It was never helpful to hear. I felt labeled based on his own annoyance with my peculiarity. My mom discouraged him from having me tested.

Everyone in town and on the news was talking about the expected storms. The El Niño effect was what my uncle studied, but the storms never came. We had drought, a little rain, and more drought. We parked at the top of the bluff and headed down to the tidal pools together. We each had our different devices for collection. I had a mason jar for some water. Morgan had a Ziploc baggie and a shovel. We didn't seem very scientific, but we were serious about our grades. The nerd ran strong in our veins. Spencer was a kindred spirit when it came to doing it right—we were all focused on our projects and no distractions. The ocean had a different plan.

At the edge of the rocks there was a shallow shelf. Just a little further out it went deep—very deep. Some divers liked to pick this spot to enter the water, hoping to get a view of something without having to go too far from their safety zone of the shore. Spencer saw it first: an orca spyhopping. He lost his footing a bit when he rubbed his eyes, making sure he saw what he thought he saw. He quietly moved toward Morgan and tugged at his shirt, not looking from the orca. Spencer whispered, hoping not to scare it away (as if that were possible).

"Looook right there. At the edge—where the shelf ends." Morgan met the gaze of the orca and held his breath, trying not to scream. The orca's head rested barely out of the water. If it weren't for its prominent white markings, he might have missed it altogether. I was closer to the edge of the water than either of them when Spencer first noticed our company. I noticed Spencer, standing suddenly tense and motionless, staring out toward the water. I followed his gaze and witnessed the whale stalking him as he reached out to Morgan, but I didn't react. Mesmerized, I stared at the glittering water surrounding the orca. I felt like I was missing something. There was something else there. Within seconds of this thought, another orca appeared slightly behind the first one. It dove into the water and then gently emerged beside the first orca—still and watching us.

Spencer took out his phone and began taking pictures. The wind picked up. The waves crashed against the rocks, and the water seemed to swell. The orcas appeared motionless. Clouds covered the small part of the sky we stood under. A storm wasn't brewing—it was here. The sky opened up, and the rain fell hard on all three of us. Morgan, the wise one, grabbed my hand.

"Let's get out of here. Back up the rocks before it gets too slippery." As he clutched my hand, one orca breached and smacked the water with its tail. A tidal wave of sea water and foam came rushing toward us. Morgan positioned himself halfway between two shielding rocks and pulled me close to him. I dropped my mason jar, and it crashed into the rocks. A shard cut Morgan on the hand. Suddenly both orcas breached, and another more powerful tidal wave crashed, knocking me off my feet and knocking Spencer into the water. Morgan shoved me behind him and edged cautiously toward the water. Spencer tried to swim back to the rocks but couldn't. He was captured by a rip current.

"Spencer, swim sideways to the rocks—you're in a riptide!" Spencer, a strong swimmer, cut through the dangerous current sideways and made his way back to the rocks. Morgan reached his hand out to guide him up. I stood shielded behind one of the larger rocks. At the base of my feet was a tide pool. A shimmering sparkly item glistened at the bottom of the pool—an ancient pearly comb with a green patina. I reached down and picked it up. Time stopped. The spray froze in the air. Morgan and Spencer stood motionless mid-rescue, teetering on the edge of the ocean. In front of me was the siren from the cave, half-bird/half-human, perched on the rock next to me.

She (I could see from her upper torso that it was a female) glared at me and spoke.

"Do not scream nor attack me again."

I did neither. I started humming and chanting, "You're not here—if you are here—go away." I closed each eye one at a time, then took turns looking with only one eye open. I clenched my jaw, held my breath, and closed both eyes, hoping that it would once again vanish. I chanted more quietly to myself.

"My brain is making order out of chaos. This is not real. May need therapy. Order out of chaos." The siren moved very close and stood with its webbed feet, which I had remembered as talons, very close. She stared straight into my eyes.

"You're not very brave, are you?" Then the creature looked over at my brother. "I like him. I was hoping you had a bit more of that in you. It's me and you, Lutey."

"So now even my delusional fantasies like my brother more than me. That's messed up." I pinched myself. I realized I was standing in the tide pool now and I was being pinched by something else. Oysters were attaching themselves to my feet and legs. Oh, the dream. I must have hit my head again or really suffered brain trauma when I was at the falls. Deep breaths. Deep breaths.

"This is no fantasy. You're being called." The siren hummed a sweet, soft song. I was instantly calmer.

"Take the comb. Hide it. From now until I see you again. Listen to the stories you are told. Especially about rainbows." I was frustrated by this cryptic directive from my new imaginary bird friend.

"Come on. If you're my subconscious, just spit it out already. I don't have the time to sit on a couch in therapy." The siren shook her head. The oysters detached and flew off. The spray was once again active, and Spencer was safely on the rock. The whales breached and swam away.

I was still holding the comb. I shoved it in my pocket. It was getting dark. Soon we wouldn't be able to see how to get back to our safe entry point, so we hurried, helping each other back up the path.

We each checked each other out for injuries. We were all fine, but shaken. "Guys, it's late. I'm just going to go home," Spencer said.

Morgan nodded. "Yeah. Weird stuff, man. Home. Good idea." Spencer took off on his skateboard.

Morgan carried his board. His small cut was bleeding.

"Why don't you let me ride Butter," he said. "You sit on the handlebars." He put his skateboard in the basket. I positioned myself between the tire and basket in a little notch. Morgan pedaled us home.

"Let's not tell Mom and Dad that we had such a close call. Okay?" I nodded my head in agreement, but I was still bewildered by the whole encounter.

"What do you think was happening out there?"

"I don't know, but I don't think those whales like us or our family. There goes my dream of being a marine biologist."

"Yeah, weird." The pearl comb dug into my thigh. "Hey, we're almost home. I think I want to walk the rest of the way. This handlebar doesn't feel so great."

Our house, like a shining beacon of safety and comfort, was within sight. Inside, my mother was curled up on the couch watching her favorite cooking show. Morgan and I snuggled up on each side of her. When I thought of the perfect moment, this was it. These two people were my world. I loved my dad, but I would do anything for my mother. She had a hold on my heart like nothing else in this world. Her illness, her recovery, her being in any state near me was what mattered. I knew my brother worried about me being too much of a hermit and not exploring friendships outside of our cousin Brooke, but I felt whole and fulfilled with this unit right here. I never wanted it to change.

Chapter 5

That night I dreamt of the weird bird creature and the pearl comb but also of a wonderful visit with the orcas deep under the waves. In my dream, I was once again at the edge of the slippery rocks with the orcas watching us. I was wearing the pearl comb in my hair. The siren sang that gentle tune she had hummed on the rocks earlier. At first I couldn't understand her words. Then I recognized them. They were a part of me already.

"Go in, dive deep, swim far." She was echoing bits of my favorite Emerson quote. "Swim far, so you shall come back with self-respect, with new power." It was all muddled up, but I could hear it speak to my soul as it had done the first time I read the words.

"Be not the slave to your own past—plunge into the sublime seas. Dive deep."

So I did. I dove off of the rocks and swam up to the orcas. The closest whale nudged me and held out a fin. I grabbed it and thrust myself onto the back of the whale, and he submerged and swam quickly below the surface. Down we went into the darkness, past the cove, out into the ocean. We emerged inside the curl of a deep sea wave and glided. We glided through the wave and went down once again. Straight down following the light. Submerged so far below the sky that the light was coming from the ocean floor, not from above. The whale stopped swimming and flipped me off his back. Bewildered, I floated aimlessly, until a dozen sea turtles of all shapes and sizes quickly surrounded me. Their shells glittered and reflected the illumination in the distance. I swam on my own toward the glimmer. The turtles swam by my side and swirled around me, keeping me on the path. They reached an area of dense ancient coral and slowed their pace.

Finally, they opened their circle, allowing a cluster of pink and purple seahorses to lead the way. My escorts clung to me, guided me, and rested in my hair. It was a long journey for their little bodies. I finally reached the blue-green light that illuminated the entire ocean floor. Dozens of mermaid statues like the one I had seen in Solvang dotted the undersea landscape and highlighted a path to an underwater grotto. Each statue shimmered with its adornments—shiny jewelry, crowns, pearls, and gold coins lay at their bases. A giant clam shell, open and empty, sat at the entrance to the grotto. Inside the sea was shallow, and now just to my waist, around my legs and feet. I walked out of the water onto the craggy sides of the grotto.

A body floated by, face down as I had been under the falls. Then hundreds of bloated, floating bodies entered the grotto, all motionless, being carried by the subtle movement of the water. One by one they either sank or floated out of the grotto. One figure was familiar. I waded between the bodies, unfazed by their cold blue skin touching mine as I tried to swim out to reach the familiar corpse. I noticed a fine bracelet on her wrist and held her hand in mine. I gently flipped the body over. Her face was scratched and her veins were bulging, but she was still recognizable. This was my Aunt Mallory's watery grave.

I needed to bring her to the surface, even though it was so far away. I grabbed hold of her hand and guided her body out of the grotto. I looked around for the sea horses, turtles, or whales. There were no sea creatures, just the statues. I started swimming straight to the surface, tugging at Aunt Mallory, but she wouldn't rise. She was sinking, and I was sinking. I clutched at her hand and the bracelet. The bracelet came off in my hand, and Mallory swirled and sank quickly. The moment our bodies separated, a gigantic sea turtle swam beneath me and lifted me to the surface. And I woke. I was clutching the pearl comb and not the bracelet.

Morgan knocked gently on my door as he opened it. "You awake?"

Still a little disoriented, I nodded.

"I need to talk about last night." He sat down at the foot of my bed and lovingly touched my arm. "I'm worried about us." He had my attention.

"Why?"

He nervously played with one of his dark curly locks. "Because, I think we have that twin thing."

I chuckled, not sure where he was going with this angle. "What do you mean? Twin thing."

He just stared at me. He put a hand lovingly on my leg, which was still under the blankets. Then I felt it. I thought I heard it, but I was looking at him and his mouth wasn't moving.

"Did you dream of Aunt Mallory last night?"

I nodded and spoke aloud. "Did you just ask me something?"

"Yes, yes, I did. And from your response, you heard me."

I leapt out of bed and wrung my hands nervously. "You know this is one of my greatest fears, right? I don't need you in my head."

"I know. I think I've been in there for a while. Not all the time. But I hear things."

I felt short of breath and exposed. "What kinds of things?"

"Well, I know that you worry about Mom a lot and that you aren't my greatest fan. Oh, and that you have seriously strong feelings for Spencer."

"Is that why he's your new best friend?" I wondered.

Morgan decided now was a good time to embrace me. "It's not all the time, Muri. It's like flashes. I was up early this morning and I kept seeing an image of Aunt Mallory."

I gave in to his hug and sobbed. "It was awful. I dreamt of her, I saw her. She was dead in the ocean."

We sat down together on the edge of the bed. He wiped my tears. "I know last night was scary, but we're not going to die the way Mallory did. There were weird coincidences to what happened with her and Uncle Nohea, but I looked it up. Most of that is just normal whale behavior. We were actually lucky to see any of it. They must have liked us. They weren't trying to kill us."

I wanted to see if the string and the can worked both ways. Could I think something to him that I wanted him to hear? Or could he just get bits and pieces of whatever I was thinking? Would I start to feel his pain, too?

"Should we tell Mom and Dad?"

He shook his head. *"No, I don't think so. I think we need to see if it's a forever thing or just a fluke. You know, like tied into the eclipse that's happening next week or some other weird event."*

I jumped up and squealed. "Wow! This is crazy! I wonder why I can't see or hear anything in your mind unless you ask me a question."

"I don't know. They really are just flashes, though. Unless you're including me in a thought, I don't hear the whole thing. I wasn't sure it was real until we had dinner last night. I knew it was something we were sharing."

"What now?"

"Nothing. There's really no reason for it. I'd kind of like my head space back, free of whatever nervous thoughts you're having,"

"I don't appreciate you categorizing them as nervous." He didn't need to read my mind to know that he had wounded and annoyed me. I shoved him out of my room. Then I stopped him for a moment.

"Have you seen—I mean in my mind—a half bird/half-human creature? It's kind of been plaguing my dreams since the waterfalls." He gave me a half-smile of relief.

"It's a siren. I didn't know if it was coming from your mind or mine."

My mom greeted us with a warm morning smile as we walked into the kitchen. "Pancakes, kiddos. I tried my hand at aebleskivers!"

We shared another wonderful breakfast with our parents. Now that my mom was feeling better, we could see the return to the good old days. Family meals together, fun conversation, future planning, and sighs of relief. My father was even talking of getting a puppy! Morgan and I had been pressing him for a furry friend for the last five years, but he thought it would be too much work for everyone (primarily him).

Today's topic was talk of a big art show of his next week. Lots of metal, plenty of iron, and lots of recognition. This was the event that might make his name internationally recognized. The big dream (even though he had never traveled out of the country) was to be desirable to a European university and take the whole family abroad. This morning he was talking about Colin and how he was actually the nephew of someone or other at the University of Edinburgh.

My big thought was: *How does a puppy work into that scenario?* Morgan, who wanted nothing ruining his chance at man's best friend, chimed in.

"By the time Dad would get anything situated, it wouldn't be a puppy anymore." My mom and dad looked at Morgan because it seemed like he had just done the ultimate non-related blurt. He realized that I hadn't spoken the thought and got up suddenly, nervous about how he would control this in his brain. Although I didn't hear a single one of his thoughts, I felt them all. Crap. I did have empathy for him. I hated knowing how he felt now that I felt it, too. I had been having trouble dealing with my roller coaster of emotions, and now I had to process his, too.

I hopped on Butter and rode to the beach on my own. I wanted to clear my head. So far, I connected to my brother and his emotions only if I was near him. I didn't even know where he was. This is how we spent most of our free days—as far away from each other as possible. The constant presence of the other one was draining. I rode to the beach, but past where we had been the night before. I was hoping to see Brooke catching an early- morning wave with the rest of her surfer friends. I parked my bike at the edge of the state beach with the rest of the morning beach lovers and trudged through the sand to where Brooke always set up. She wasn't there. Why didn't I have a phone? I realized that my father had never given it back to me. I hadn't missed it until this moment.

Brooke's house was farther than I wanted to ride on my bike, so I traversed the unpleasant sand back to my bike and rode home. I would get my phone back and then track her down. As I rode past the cliffs on my way our special tidal pool spot I saw Brooke, and she wasn't alone. Brooke and Colin were standing on the cliff. He pointed out to the open sea, and she nodded her head, listening intently. He must have been showing her those sea spray rainbows. I had never seen one. Either way, I was excited to catch up with her without having to travel all the way back home. I stopped and called out to her, but she couldn't hear me over the sound of the crashing waves and ocean. I left my bike near the base and climbed up the side, but froze when I saw Colin lean in and kiss Brooke. My stomach dropped like an elevator crashing to the ground. My face burned, and I could feel the heat rising from the bottom of my belly as it traveled upward. Dizzy and sweaty, I witnessed their lips meet. I could have turned and given them their privacy, but I screamed in horror. This time, she heard me. Brooke gasped when she saw me and rushed toward me. She was on me before I knew it and grabbed my arm forcefully. I already didn't know who she was.

"What are you doing here?" She continued her firm grasp on my arm. I shook off her hold.

"Chill. What's up with the body grab? I came to watch you surf this morning. Like I always do. What are you doing here?" Brooke glanced back up the cliff. Colin didn't look shocked or attempt to come our way. He appeared unfazed by my presence or what I had witnessed. Brooke patted me on the shoulder.

"Uh, hey, sorry. Colin is helping me understand what could have happened to my mom." I looked skeptical.

"By kissing you? Does your dad know that you're hanging out with him? Why didn't you tell me you were into him?"

Brooke blushed. "That was unexpected. He was just sharing everything he knows with me about these types of occurrences and what causes them."

"I'm not tracking with you. Occurrences?"

"When the sea takes someone. Intentionally." Now I had just experienced a bizarre dream, meeting a siren (real or imagined), discovering telepathic powers with my twin brother, but in this moment, I thought she was terrifying. Her eyes were flat and lacked expression. In the past there was a glint of charm and a raised eyebrow that she included in every response—especially if I was spiraling. Brooke was trying to explain the unexplainable, but it was this moment that was a puzzle. Her mother was part of a weird storm and sea life event. She was just unlucky. Why was Brooke suddenly clinging to this idea?

"Your mom," I hesitated. "Your mom was just unlucky."

Brooke grabbed me by my shoulders and shook me hard. "She wasn't unlucky."

This made me mad. I was sorry for Brooke, but I had a bad feeling about Colin and this story he was selling her. Then I did it. I repeated something I had heard my father say. As it was coming out of my mouth, I knew I shouldn't have been saying it and that I couldn't take it back once it leapt out.

"She was. Even her name means unlucky."

Brooke shoved me to the ground and shook her head. We didn't realize that Colin had climbed down from the cliff to intervene. He had overheard what I said. He reached out a hand to me, helping me up off the ground. I dusted the dirt from my pants. I hated getting the earth on me in any form—sand, dirt, mud—although mud was the most desirable of the three. I knew that didn't make much sense, but the dryness of the other textures bothered me. So wet mud, not drying clay mud, on me. My brain buzzed as I categorized and rationalized the level of earth material that I was okay with—Play-Doh was okay, but that's wheat, so not really clay. Brooke could tell that she had triggered my sensory issue. I could barely hear what Colin was saying. She just snarled at me in disgust.

"That is unkind what you said, but not untrue. Mallory means ill-fated." Brooke's eyes filled with tears. Colin put his arm around her, comforting her.

"I'm sorry. It's just the literal meaning to her name." I focused on Colin.

"How do you know that?"

"It's another area of interest of mine. Just like your name means bright sea."

"What are you, an expert on everything? So what's this grand theory you're sharing with my cousin? You know she's been through a lot."

"Yes, I know. Remember, I'm not the one who just told her the meaning of her mother's name. I was the one confirming that it was true." He reached his hand down to Brooke's and gripped it gently.

"So. What's the deal? I saw you putting the moves on her. You're too old, don't you think?" If I could have read Brooke's aura it would have been a murky red. Her continued gaze had heat to it.

"None of your business. Colin, let's go. Let's see what my father has discovered." Colin looked at me with kind caring. The hair on the back of my neck stood up and my skin felt like it was crawling.

"A storm is coming, Muriel. Please stay out of the water." Just then my brother and Spencer skated by and stopped. Morgan could sense the tense situation.

"Everything okay?"

Brooke lashed out.

"Your sister is on my last nerve. She's gone, aggro." Next to Spencer and Morgan, the slightly older Colin looked tiny and thin. He wouldn't have a chance in a fight. I was hoping there would be a fight. Everything about this guy told me not to trust him. Morgan watched Brooke carefully, suspiciously. I could feel the question marks in his mind.

"What exactly is going on here?"

Colin stepped up for an answer. "Brooke and I were just discussing my research and some similarities with cases like her mother's. Her father and I have discovered some compelling information." This intrigued Spencer.

"How does your rainbow spectrum spray thing figure into her mom's boating accident?"

Colin adjusted his glasses and cleared his throat slightly. "My other area of research, mermaids and weather." Spencer shook his head. "Yeah, uh, that doesn't seem really helpful to this family situation."

Colin was unfazed. "I'm just helping her learn the truth. Or the possibilities that exist."

Morgan pleaded with me, "Come on, Muri. Spencer and I are going to check out the new fish taco stand. Let her do what she needs to do."

I looked at Brooke's angry face, Colin's weirdly placid expression, and Morgan's urging glance, and then decided to say one more thing—since I had a reputation for not letting well enough alone. That's why Morgan was trying to extricate me from the situation. I fell into the trap of having *Wizard of Oz* moments, "and your little dog, too!" Morgan once told my mother, "Muri doesn't just burn a bridge, she sets the lake on fire." I was trying to contain myself but just couldn't. I didn't always use the best judgment.

"I'm not going anywhere until I've got some better answers. They were just kissing. That's so many levels of wrong. He's filling her head with ideas that her mother was 'taken' or something. This guy's a nut."

Spencer looped his arm through mine and tried to escort me down the path back to my bike. "Let's go, Muri."

I shoved him off. "I'm not the mental case here! She's just so desperate to have a reason for Aunt Mallory's death. There is no reason. She's dead. It was horrible. She's dead, probably long ago eaten, maybe by the very fish at the taco stand. You'll probably get better insight from eating one of those fish tacos then talking to this dude."

Okay, so we will instantly all agree this was not my finest moment. Maybe the worst—but I was trying to get her to see reason. This guy was trouble. In that moment I was feeling bad that I had said something so harsh, but also rationalizing and validating my behavior. I was so preoccupied in trying to assuage my guilt that I didn't see Brooke come at me. Oh, and she came at me hard. The next thing I knew, I was on the ground and Brooke was on top of me, literally pulling my hair out. She also landed a well-deserved punch on my face. But this wasn't Brooke. This wasn't her temper—it was more like mine. Luckily this was the first time that my mouthing off had resulted in physical violence, but it was inevitable. People warned me upon occasion.

Colin was the first person to my rescue. He pulled Brooke off me and tried to calm her. I again focused on the dirt on my clothing and not so much the surrounding people.

"She doesn't understand. She hasn't looked at the research and other accounts of similar things happening." He spoke on my behalf to Brooke. Brooke took a deep breath. She seemed zoned out and walked away from all of us. Colin talked calmly and softly, directing his message to us, and I thought to me in particular. "Give us a chance to share with you what we know. Go get your fish tacos. We're meeting her dad at the university library in an hour. Meet us there."

My nostrils were flaring. Morgan and Spencer could tell that I hadn't calmed down one bit. Morgan touched my hand and then spoke into my mind, taking up all the space of my own thoughts. I could feel his fear and caution. Prickly chills went up my arms and down the back of my spine. I listened. *Muriel. Let this be. Let them go. We'll figure out what to do.* Colin looked at me like he was trying to hear what Morgan was saying to me, but that couldn't be true. I took a deep breath.

"Okay."

The boys and I went to check out the new fish taco stand. As we walked, we talked about meeting Brooke and her dad at the library and how our dad would feel about that. Just by listening, were we conspiring against him and his belief system (which was ours as well)? Spencer wanted to hear more about it all. He was still processing the events from the night before and thought maybe some of what was being said could be true. The only thing I thought could be true was the weather.

"The weather does weird things to people. It could do weird things to animals. I could be swayed toward a weather scenario."

Then Spencer spoke up. "Even after what happened last night and what Morgan told me is happening to you guys?"

I glared at Morgan. "What did you tell him was happening?"

Morgan shrugged. "I needed to tell someone else. You know, a control person. Someone objective."

I had wanted to tell my mother; I guess having another person on our side, believing what was beginning to seem like mass hysteria, would help us sort through the facts.

Spencer chimed in. "I won't tell anyone. You can trust me."

I took a deep breath. "On some level I know that. Even if you did throw a rock at my head."

Spencer laughed. "You'll never let that go, will you?"

"Was it an accident?"

"No, I was mad at you. You abandoned our friendship. It hurt."

Victory was mine!

"I told you it was on purpose, Morgan."

Morgan nodded. "Yes, now we know. Can we just leave it forever in the past?"

"Yes." I was determined to never bring it up again. So Spencer felt that same way—abandoned.

We decided we would meet them at the library and see what they had to say, but I needed to go home first. Even though I liked to play defiant, I didn't like willfully undoing any faith my parents had in me. It was hard won, and so easily lost. Ultimately, I just wanted to be their good girl that they could be proud to say was theirs. I wanted to be calm and predictable. I wanted to endure weird smells, bright flashing lights, dirt on my clothes, and sand between my toes—but that wasn't me.

My mom sat at the piano playing a beautiful original piece. When she first met my father in college, she was still performing in recitals. She was a music major and gifted with the rare talent to create, not perform. He encouraged her to give it up if she didn't enjoy performing. I always suspected he wanted the attention for himself. Now, she played the piano and the violin when her body didn't hurt, but for herself, never for an audience. She also was not a singer. She never sang, not even lullabies to us as children. She subscribed to the Suzuki method—we were only to hear proper melodies. She believed if we heard what sounded like tone-deaf singing it would forever taint our brains. Ultimately, that meant that no one sang in our home. We listened to beautiful music, though—plenty of Chopin and Mozart. Yet my parents bonded over Miles Davis and classic surf music like the song "Green Onions." It was an odd combination, but so were they.

Other than the fact that they both enjoyed the arts (and us) they had very little in common. It surprised me to hear what types of things they had planned on parents' nights out, aka date nights. My mother, who wanted to travel extensively and had done quite a bit before she and my father started dating, liked to try exotic restaurants and listen to live music. My father only liked American cuisine—preferably Californian with a farm to table concept. If it had too many ingredients, he didn't like it. So chai was off his list forever. His preferred activity was to visit silent art galleries and museums, and he didn't like to discuss the work whenever he took us. He liked the silence. That was my preference, too, but I couldn't help but notice the differences and that she never got her way—not unless that's really what he wanted too. We went to the ocean and the beach a lot as children, but my mother never went in because she was my constant companion and I would fuss.

I idolized my mother, even though she was not the picture of female empowerment. It's like she was required to submit to my father's will. Yet... it didn't seem to bother her. It's like he always just clarified that his idea was far superior to hers. Every once in a while, he would placate her and let her have her way. She never noticed. I noticed. I noticed and resented every choice he made for her. I often suspected that the autoimmune illness resulted from her stifled will. She had enough books on the mind/body connection and healing illness that I thought she would have figured it out. She simply adored him, and her fate was in his hands. At least he was a magnanimous ruler.

I sat down next to her on the piano bench. She stopped playing and put her arm around me.

"My sweet, why so glum? Didn't you find Brooke?"

I rested my head on her shoulder. She stroked my hair and kissed the top of my head. This was my safe place. The world always seemed so harsh and lonely. My thoughts, my feelings bubbling beneath the surface, big concepts all out of sync with my peers. My brain buzzing all the time, and my senses on high alert. These were the moments I craved. There was no true silence except the silence of being in my mother's arms. Morgan could have been bitter about me being the squeaky wheel. He knew I needed more—more of her and her essence—and he seemed willing to give it. Even though I felt that I was more like my father, we were always at opposite purposes.

"She was with that Colin guy." My mother took a deep breath.

"Oh."

She sat me up and looked at me softly. She caressed my face.

"It was bound to happen at some point. She is older than you. Dating won't be the end of your special bond, sweetie. Give her a chance."

I grimaced. "It's not the concept of dating that bothers me. It's this guy. I don't like him."

My dad walked into the room. He was loaded down with pieces of iron and metalworking tools. He was starting his final push on his artwork before the big show. Even though my mother asked him nicely to change his shoes or shake off before traveling from his in-home studio to the backyard and other regions of the house—he forgot. During these intense work cycles, he unintentionally brought in shards of metal shavings and deposited them in little bits around the house. We'd all fallen victim to a shard in the foot.

"What guy?"

My mom gave him a stern look. "Mother–daughter talk, okay? Anyway, we're not talking about anything related to Muri."

My dad nodded, respecting the mother–daughter code.

"Okay, as long as she's still not harping on Spencer. I think that kid is all right."

My mom shooed him away, but first shook her head at his bundle of metal. I saw my mom's face and picked up a piece of metal that had fallen to the ground and stacked it back on my dad. He shuffled out of the room.

"Okay, maybe I am just jealous of the interest she's showing him." My mom struggled to get up from the piano bench and I helped her. She was having a relapse. I noticed the walker positioned nearby. "Let me grab it, Mom."

She laughed. "I think we are in for a few weeks of the special toilet." My mother needed the assistance of a handicapped toilet on these days because of her limited mobility. This broke my heart. Even though she handled each wave of her illness with grace and dignity, I could barely stand it. I wished I knew how to help her. I brought the walker to her and desperately needed a distraction.

"I'm meeting up with Morgan at the university for our science project research. Is there anything I can do for you before I go?"

"I've got something in the oven; can you get it out for me?"

So even her cooking would be on hold again. I pulled out the most delicious- smelling lasagna from the oven. She knew she was getting worse. She only baked the big freezable meals when she thought she was going to be letting us down. I wished she knew that her value wasn't based on dinner time. I loved her no matter what state she was in—but I couldn't tell her that. I was just compelled to leave—to get as far away from my emotions as I could.

Inside the dimly lit university library I scanned the rows of walnut-stained bookshelves for the area where Brooke's group had set up shop. In the very far back of the library, past the college-aged students, was a large round table with scattered texts and notebooks strewn about. Colin emerged from one of the stacks near the table, followed by Brooke and my uncle Nohea. He had a large heavy book in his hands that he added to the other literature on the table. They leaned over the new tome as Colin flipped through the pages. He found what he was looking for as I hung back and walked rather slowly toward them. Colin looked up suddenly and stared straight at me.

"I'm glad you came."

In this moment, in this lighting, I wondered if Colin was really in his twenties. He was somehow much older feeling to me. He adjusted his glasses as I thought about this. Brooke saw me and frowned, but her dad embraced me.

"You've got to see this, Muriel. This will change our lives."

I hugged him, but then sneered. "I highly doubt it." I was still sour from the interaction with my mother. Her situation seemed so unfair. I had to remind myself that she was alive, and I got to go home and see her after this. I tried to soften my unkind words. "But I'm interested in hearing where he's going with this."

My uncle didn't seem to notice my attitude. "I understand your skepticism. That's why I ask that whatever we share with you today, you keep to yourself for now. Your father will be a tough critic of what we are discovering."

I nodded in agreement as Morgan and Spencer located us in the back of the library. Uncle Nohea hugged Morgan, then reached out and shook Spencer's hand. Brooke just looked at everyone, her face looking unsure of whether she wanted us there. I could feel Morgan getting tense. He had a deep faith just like my father's, and this had a bit of an occult feel to it. He couldn't pinpoint why he was uncomfortable, but I could feel it. He didn't trust Colin either.

"So what is this information you wanted to share?"

Spencer, Morgan, and I stood close together at the other side of the round table. Colin slid the book he was looking at toward us. My uncle picked up another one resting on the table and put it next to us. The first book was of Bible artwork throughout the ages. The second was a book on different types of lore and the historical basis for each myth within it. The Bible artwork was a reprint of the Nuremberg Bible scene of Noah's ark. The lore book was open to a page with our name at the top of the particular tale.

My uncle grinned excitedly. "Brooke, you, and Morgan—are Lutey."

Colin shook his head. "We are still researching if Brooke is a Lutey, or if it's only those that possess the surname."

Morgan appeared agitated. "So what is that supposed to mean?"

I picked up the book and read the tale. Spencer looked closer at the book of artwork. "What is this? Is this supposed to be Noah's Ark?"

Brooke finally spoke. "Yes, that's Noah's Ark. And that's a mermaid, a merman, and what looks like a freaky mer-dog or mer-animal."

Spencer looked closer. "Crazy. A mer-animal. I've never heard of that before. Are they supposed to have gotten on the ark with Noah?"

Brooke looked at Spencer with disdain. She seemed more like an unpleasant version of me than the sweet champion I admired. Something had changed in her. My uncle came up behind me and pointed to what he felt was the important part of the story. He touched my shoulder awkwardly.

"Your ancestor, and we have confirmed through your own father's records that it is your ancestor, met a mermaid and gained powers and a curse on the Lutey family. The mermaid gave him a pearl-encrusted comb, and he made three wishes, which were all noble and gave generations these powers. But every nine years, a Lutey descendant is lost in water and their body is never discovered."

Morgan was skeptical. "Wouldn't we have heard about our family members going missing?"

Nohea laughed. "Why would you know? What relatives do you know other than Brooke and your aunt? Your family is spread out all over, and this ancestor was hundreds of years ago. This may be the first time it has touched so close."

I could barely hear anyone speaking. I just kept thinking about the pearl comb stashed back at my house. I could feel Brooke's eyes on me. I looked up to see a moment of scorn. There was something they weren't telling us.

"So what were these powers it says our family has?"

Colin fielded this question. "The old fisherman Lutey wished for the power to do good, by breaking spells to heal, and control the will of all manner of supernatural creatures, especially mermaids that might harm someone, and that each generation would have these powers."

Morgan looked frustrated. "So why do we need to know any of this fiction? Are you warning us to stay out of the water? What's the point?"

Brooke grabbed another book and slammed it down. She pointed to the illustration from another story. "We're bringing my mother back."

Spencer gasped at this. "You can't be serious?!"

Colin shut the book Brooke brought over before I got a good look at it. It looked Mexican or Mayan or something. It showed an illustration of twin boys.

"We are just learning more and exploring what options there are. The first thing we need to do is find a mermaid. With three Lutey descendants, we should be able to do it." My uncle Nohea stressed the words "three Lutey descendants." We all knew there were four. This meant they never planned to include my dad.

I took a deep breath. "I'm out. This is truly the most ridiculous conversation I've ever had. I appreciate you doing our little family lore research, but I've got a real life to live over here. Enter our DNA info into an ancestry website; I'm sure you can find some different rubes to help you."

Brooke moved closer to me like she might punch me again or something. "We're the last of the line. And what about my mom? You don't care?"

I was not about to be intimidated by her for one more minute. "I care. I loved your mom. I love you, but she's gone. Process it."

Morgan hung his head low and then nodded in agreement. "Aunt Mallory is in heaven. I'll say a prayer for all of you at church." Morgan grabbed my hand and walked me out of the library. Spencer was close behind us.

"Muri, where is that comb?" I forgot that he was in my head.

"In my room."

Spencer looked puzzled. "What's in your room?"

Morgan stopped and talked quietly to Spencer. "This is where we have to part ways today, Spence."

My brother rarely called him by that nickname, but Morgan was trying to reassure him he wouldn't be out of the loop for long. I could see there was a lot of trust between these guys—the kind of trust I used to have with Brooke. Now I would have to rely on my brother, whom I knew I could always trust even if we disagreed. Back at the house, my mother had gone to bed early and was distracting herself from the pain by watching her favorite British baking show. My father was still sequestered in his metals studio.

Morgan and I rushed to my room and grabbed the comb. I held it out to him—our hands were both on the comb for a moment, and it glowed. I wanted to drop it, but Morgan reached out and held it tight with my hand in his. I could feel the warmth radiate from the comb through our bodies.

"Drop the comb," a melodic voice urged. Startled, we did just that and dropped the comb to the floor. We looked around the room for the source of the voice. My siren friend had returned, and this time was not in a frozen moment or a dream. She was here, and I hadn't hit my head. Oh, and I had a witness: my brother.

I whispered softly, "Are you seeing what I'm seeing?"

He nodded. "Uh-huh."

"Now, now, children. Relax. You've both had your hands on the comb. The die has been cast. Let's just move forward from here." The siren sang this softly and ominously. We were so unaccustomed to singing in our home that it was the most unsettling thing.

"Can you please just speak and not sing?" Morgan requested. This offended the siren.

"Singing is what I do. You don't find it pleasing at all? It doesn't make you want to listen to me or do as I say?"

We both laughed. "No, the opposite. I sort of want to cringe and tune you out. Sorry." I was genuinely apologetic, because the siren seemed hurt by the comment.

She said, "Well, it's simple enough. You are immune, so why should I bother? My name is Calliope."

Morgan got his first good look at Calliope. She had a small birdlike frame, and her shiny feathers and scaly bird feet seemed different each time I saw her. Her face was softer than it was in my dream. She was obviously a woman but had a very youthful face. She was either as old as me or a hundred years older, age—unidentifiable. She was timeless, magical, and beautiful. I wasn't looking at her with fear this time and could imagine how I must have seemed to her the first time we met in the cave under the waterfall. That reminded me—the waterfall. What was happening there?

"So why did I see you at the waterfall? What did you do to me?"

She scoffed. "I did nothing to you. I called out for assistance, and you didn't help me. I wanted to see what you would do." She showed off a little patch of shimmery feathers that seemed to be regenerating. "You did the opposite and assaulted me." Then she turned on Morgan. "And you. Those fish were trying to rouse your sister, and you started kicking and screaming at them."

"Okay, okay, we've got it. So we freaked out. What do you want from us now?" "Why were you testing us? What do you want?" I looked suspiciously at her innocent-looking face.

"Oh, my dear Luteys—it's you who should tell me what you want. I am under your power now."

"What the what? So that powers nonsense has some truth to it? And what would we want?"

"There are many things that can be done—but in a hundred years no Lutey has intentionally used their power. The knowledge was lost to your clan."

"My cousin thinks we can help her find a mermaid and help her get her mother back who drowned at sea."

Calliope shook her head. "No, that cannot be done."

Morgan shrugged. "Well, that's it then. I can't think of anything else that might be on the agenda."

I sat down in a chair by my desk and pulled out my notepad. I may have mentioned that I was not only an artist, but also a nerd. I took notes. I loved any opportunity to have a pen and paper in my hands. It may have been part of my need for a positive tactile experience. I liked how smooth the pens were between my fingers. I felt grounded when I could put things that were floating around my brain onto concrete paper where I could see the words and make sense of them. I wrote down all the dreams that haunted me and all the feeling I couldn't contain. I was a journaler.

"So it's not possible ... why? Because mermaids aren't real? Because we don't have that kind of power?" I was ready to scribble down whatever our feathered friend had to share.

"Mermaids are real. That is how you and your brother have powers. Yet, your powers can only be used for good. That is the bargain your Lutey grandfather from long ago made." Even though Morgan was chatting with a half-bird, half-female he seemed to think mermaids were preposterous. I could feel his skepticism filling the room.

"So how do they exist?"

"Asking about their existence is an esoteric question. Are you asking about a creation story, or are you asking about why you don't believe that they exist?" Calliope climbed up on my bed and fiddled with the pillows and stuffed animals placed around the headboard. (Yes, I still have a few treasured stuffies.) She pulled the comforter back slightly and slid her webbed talons beneath the sheets. A bird under my sheets was not my ideal scenario. She sighed as if this were the height of luxury. I wanted to ask her to get off my bed, but I couldn't. I wanted to hear what she was going to say to Morgan. I didn't want to upset her. Morgan watched her climb under the sheet and knew what I was thinking. He also didn't want to rock the boat.

"I guess I want an origin story."

She continued to make herself comfortable. "Do you have tea or something warm to drink? It's quite drafty in this room. Once we work that out, I will tell you all you want to know."

My father knocked at the door—a quick double knock—as he opened it. It surprised him to see both of us in my room. Our eyes darted to the bed. No Calliope.

"Oh, good. I was going to ask Muri if she had seen you. I need help to move a couple of pieces to my truck. We're getting closer, guys! Can you imagine—we could move to Paris or Milan. I saw two job postings at universities over there."

Morgan got up and could feel my disappointment and my thoughts.

This was the first time in a while I'd heard him try to put my dad in check. He might have been doubly disappointed because our bird had flown the coop.

"Yeah, that's great, Dad. I'd be happy for you—but what about Mom? What does her doctor say? Have you even asked?"

My dad frowned. "Can't we just have one moment that's focused on possibility and not limitations?"

"I sure hope you just didn't call my mother a limitation." I pursed my lips together and turned around in my chair. "By the way—your brother-in-law and niece are still convinced that something supernatural was involved in Aunt Mallory's loss at sea. Can you please shut it down? It's stressing me out."

My dad looked angered by both comments. I couldn't tell which made him more enraged: the accusation I made about him disparaging my mother, or that my uncle was once again desecrating his sister's memory. I only felt guilty about one comment. I knew what they had said in the library had some truth to it—but I wanted it all to go away. I really didn't want Calliope to return. I hoped to have nothing to write in my notebook. It surprised Morgan that I came clean about the conversation in the library. He knew that confrontation would only bring more trouble to our doorstep. He looked at me disapprovingly. He pushed a thought into my mind.

"Mistake. Why did you involve Dad? We could have made it go away on our own." I shrugged and said nothing more.

As soon as my dad loaded up the truck, he went to confront Nohea. He wanted to cut off the head of the conspiracy. He felt he owed it to his niece to make sure they lived in reality. While my dad was confronting my uncle, Brooke came to confront me. My mother was up looking for something to eat with her pills and intercepted Brooke before she made it to my room. I could hear their conversation from the hall. I slipped out of my room and lurked at the end of the hall. I was trying to decide if I would hide, make a break for it, or face her.

"I'm glad you're here, Brooke." My mom stood between Brooke and my location. Brooke tried to move past my mom, but my mom held her ground with the adult parental authority.

"Is Muriel in her room?"

"I honestly don't know. I was resting. She may have gone out with her father."

"No, he's with my dad." She again made a move to pass my mother. I decided I was going to run if she made it into the hall.

"I'm glad you're here, because I want to talk to you about Colin. I think he's slightly old for you." This stopped Brooke in her tracks. Her face grew cold and fierce.

"What did Muriel say?"

My mom put her frail hand on Brooke's shoulder. "Just that she thought you guys were developing a maybe inappropriate friendship."

Brooke looked at the pills in my mother's hands and lashed out, brushing my mother's other hand off of her.

"Take your pills, Lorelei. Worry about yourself. My mother will be back soon enough. I don't need you pretending to be one. I almost feel sorry for Muriel and Morgan. I don't know what's worse—to have an actual missing mother or one right in front of you that's vanished."

Lorelei looked pierced and shaky. I wanted to leap from the shadows and confront my cousin. I wanted to make her suffer for being so cruel to my mother. My mother paused for a moment, caught between wanting to say something to Brooke and listening to her words. She stood motionless for a moment and then took her pills.

"You are right. I'm not your mother. Good night, Brooke. I need to rest." She turned and walked into her bedroom. I didn't leap. I watched my mother walk away. I saw her safely tucked into her room, and then I emerged from the shadows.

"You need to leave my house."

"Why did you tell your dad? You knew he would try to stop us."

"Stop you from what? Wishing on a star? Dreaming of a mythical mermaid? You're crazy."

"Colin already knows where one is."

"We all do—the ocean and his imagination."

"No, this evil fish is on land. We will return her to the ocean, and I'll get my mother back."

"You are nuts and frankly not very nice anymore. I'm sure Colin is a good kisser, but to give up all of your own common sense? I didn't realize how desperate you were."

It was about to get physical when Morgan and my dad walked through the door. Brooke latched on to my shirt and was winding up for the blow. She pulled back when she saw the guys. I shook it off like I wasn't terrified of another beatdown.

"Did you get her dad straightened out? This mental case has wiped out one too many times and will believe anything."

Morgan looked shocked by my comment. "Easy, Muriel, that's too harsh!" I noticed my dad's bloodied hand, and his face had a bruise on it.

Brooke noticed, too. "Did you hit my dad? Did he tell you the truth about everything?"

Morgan shook his head. "There wasn't much talking, and yes, there were punches thrown. I'm pretty sure we won't be having Thanksgiving together this year, or maybe any year."

Brooke rushed out of the house. "You're all fools."

"I'm glad she's gone. You should have heard how she talked to Mom."

I got some ice for Dad's hand. He smiled. "We need a family reset."

Chapter 6

The next morning, my father had the entire family dressed and ready for church. He had let us and Brooke down. He was in charge of our spiritual upbringing. He was supposed to be the head of our household and guide us the way his father had guided him. How were we even being exposed to these ideas of the occult? Nohea had converted when he and Aunt Mallory married, but what did that really mean? All of them had rebelled against going to church regularly. It was the practice of it they had railed against. There was always something better to do. My father was a believer, so that was enough, he thought. His children would get it by osmosis and from the example of my parents being good people and living a good life. He had failed, and now here we sat in the third pew on the left.

We were Christmas and Easter Christians, and we had always been okay with that. Morgan and I could feel the stares. We were sitting in some devoted churchgoers' regular seats. My father got up to light a candle. My mother looked intently at the hymn books, reading the music with great interest. Morgan and I exchanged telepathic barbs about how lame our father was being and how nice the stained glass was. I also wondered about the Bible images we saw with the mermaid. My stomach turned a bit when I thought about Brooke's words about an evil fish being on land. My very best friend and the person I had wanted to be for the last six months seemed sinister to me. Maybe I would pray. It couldn't hurt, right? I at least needed to do more research. We needed Calliope to return. This thought made my stomach do another flip-flop.

Morgan was thumbing through his Bible and looking things up on his phone. He pulled up the image of Noah and the Ark with the mermaids. He was trying to find any scriptural reference and couldn't. He hid his phone when my father got back to the pew. One word had come up on his search and he projected it into my mind: nephilim. What did that mean? I had never heard or read that word before. Did it have something to do with mermaids or Calliope?

The service was long, and we were out of practice. My mother enjoyed listening to the hymns, and this church had white-gloved bell-ringers, which was a treat. I got antsy while sitting on the hard, wooden pew. I wished we could bring cushions like at the stadium games. A young girl with an amazing voice was a musical guest at this service. She sang "Ave Maria," and as her voice filled up every cell in my body, the chatter and worry in my head floated away. Not even Morgan could penetrate my thoughts. I closed my eyes, took a deep cleansing breath, and listened to the words.

In this private meditation and moment of contemplative prayer, my mother leaned over and whispered in my ear. "When I die, please play this song for me. It moves me the way it moves you."

I opened my eyes. The thought of my mother dying sent sickening shock waves through my body. Then the next feeling surprised me. I was overwhelmed with compassion for Brooke. I knew in my heart that she was hurting. If there was anything I could do, I should help her. Maybe with the three of us we could help her somehow. Yet, my gut overrode my do-gooder moment. My gut said "No." The song was over, and Morgan was eavesdropping on my thoughts. I reached out and held my mother's hand and ignored his declaration: *"We can't help Brooke!"* I would make my own decision on that. I might need to help my cousin. If our powers, whatever they were, were here to help people and for good—then we must step up and do something. Calliope was testing me by the waterfalls, and I had failed. Maybe this was just another test I was failing. I knew that my mother wasn't going to die. She might not be healthy, but she would not die anytime soon. Brooke had already lost her mother. My father had lost his sister, and Uncle Nohea would never be the same. They were searching for answers. I should search, too.

Back home, I sat on the bed with the comb in my hand. It did nothing. Morgan quickly appeared, because he could sense what I was doing.

"I want to hear what Calliope knows about what happened to Aunt Mallory. If we ask about that, we will help Brooke. Then we can all get back to normal."

"Muri, even if we have some sort of powers, you heard it just like I did. We are cursed as much as we are blessed. We need to not mess with it anymore."

"What if it were Mom? I know you understand why she's looking for answers. It's changed her. I don't feel the old Brooke anymore. I don't know if it's Colin or just the stages of grief, but that girl is not right."

Morgan finally agreed to summon Calliope again. We put both of our hands on the comb. We felt the energy transmit through us and the comb glowed. Calliope appeared, singing "Ave Maria." This immediately disturbed me.

"Why are you singing that song?"

"Because I think it is lovely."

Her singing also disturbed Morgan. "Were you at the church today?"

Calliope sang, "Maria Gratia plena, Maria Gratia plena Ave, Avea Dominus. I'm with you now until this is over."

"What does that mean? Were you at the church?"

"It means that when you are thinking about me—I'm with you. You can't see me, but I'm with you. Once you called me with the comb, I'm here until this journey is over."

Morgan didn't like this one bit. He believed we had some control. If we chose not to call her again with the comb, then we could be done with it all. It was now clear to him we were not in control, and he was afraid. I could feel the fear welling up in him, but he beat it down because at his core he *was* brave—the bravest person I would ever meet. He did the only thing he could think of to expel an evil spirit or other horrible thing that was trying to take over our lives and our wills. He had heard it before but never thought it was a real phrase to use until now.

"Get thee behind me, Satan." Morgan had gone old-school Bible. He pulled out the phrase from the deep recesses of his mind.

Calliope fell to the floor laughing. "It's been a while since I've had a great laugh. Thank you." I didn't appreciate her laughing at my brother.

"If you don't want that nicely grown-in feather patch to get plucked, you'd better start explaining yourself. What the hell is going on?" Morgan was crestfallen. Calliope stopped laughing.

"I'm not from the devil, and I am no form of evil. I am a child of a fallen angel. And since God is good, he did not punish us children for merely being born. I'm what's called a nephilim and was born as a siren. My other nephilim cousins are mermaids, selkies, undines, merfairies, merangels, and sea creatures like the Naga and dolphins."

"That sounds like a lot of crazy talk, but you are definitely not human so get to it—why are you bothering us?" My tone wasn't welcoming.

"I take offense to your claiming that I'm bothering you. Humans are always trying to blame us for something or other or just denying our existence."

I was taking notes now of all the things she had been saying. I circled back to one comment. "We don't deny dolphins exist."

Calliope pursed her lips together in disappointment. "Yes, dolphins refuse to be ignored. They have such a love–hate relationship with mankind. The whole Cetacean family is confused about how to interact with you."

All of our recent research for the science fair was paying off. Cetaceans are whales and dolphins. But now that we were clear on her entire nephilim community, we had no more answers than we did before.

"What about this curse on our family? If you aren't evil, then why is someone from our family line taken every nine years?"

Calliope spoke quietly and sincerely. "I didn't say there wasn't evil in this world. I just said that I wasn't evil."

"And what about the curse?"

"I honestly don't know. The merfolk have their own society and reasons for doing things. Since God entrusted them to guard Noah's Ark during the flood, they have assumed the role as leaders of the nephilim and don't consult the rest of us."

Morgan pulled up the picture of the Nuremberg Bible on his phone and looked closely at the picture. "You can't be serious that there are mer-dogs." It surprised me that after all the shocking and unbelievable information that Calliope had shared with us, my brother focused on whether or not there were mer-dogs. Calliope nodded her head.

"Yes, mer-dogs."

"What about mer-cats?" he followed.

Calliope's face twisted with questioning eyes. "No, no mer-cats."

"Well, that's disappointing!" he sighed. I was trying not to be over-whelmed and irritated by my brother's line of questioning. I needed time to process. I still wanted to help Brooke, but I wasn't sure what that even meant.

"Have you talked to Brooke? She's a Lutey. You could just help her. Talk to her. Let her know there is nothing that we can do."

Calliope looked solemn. "I am not here because you are Luteys." She turned her head toward the sky and listened to the wind. "I must go."

With that, she was gone again. Then Morgan shouted out, "But you're not really gone, are you!" He looked at me. "I'm super creeped out."

"What do you think about talking to Brooke?" I pleaded.

"Let's wait until after Dad's show and the science fair. I don't have the time to focus on this for one more minute. I went this long without knowing any of this. I'm perfectly fine sweeping it under the rug for now."

So that's what we did—we swept it under the rug. I had to do my science project on my own, since Brooke wasn't an option. My dad spent his days and nights finishing up his pieces and having Morgan do some of the heavy lifting. My mom's health continued to decline. This was our path for the next two weeks. We didn't think about or call out to Calliope. We pretended that we could control it all if we tried hard enough. We could deal with it when we were ready. We had promised each other not to think about it. So far it was working. Denial was our best friend.

Chapter 7

Morgan and I focused on our own goals and keeping our family life going for the past week, but we deceived ourselves into thinking we could control what happened next. We were embarking upon two days that would define our lives forever.

My project for the science fair was simple. Our original hypothesis was piggybacking off of Aunt Mallory's research. The climate was changing, the oceans were getting warmer, and that was making specific species behave differently. I didn't want to create an even greater rift with my cousin, so I adjusted my project to focus on algae and not coral.

Day one—the science fair. They set the gymnasium up with dozens of individual booths. Some required special lighting or access to several outlets. Many of the students were showing the science of the total solar eclipse that would occur the following afternoon. Everyone in the science community was excited about it. Even my uncle Nohea had started talking about it months ago. They were excited to track weather changes after the eclipse. It had been about forty years since the last solar eclipse was visible in North America. The new technology would allow scientists to capture all kinds of details unknown previously. With all the science community hubbub, it was easy for students to access graphs, charts, or other illustrations to enhance their projects.

I was sure that one of them would win the fair.

My project was fairly simple. I had sea water, two types of algae, and several graphs and charts. I wasn't going for the win. I just wanted to have something to show and get a passing grade. This was unlike my normal style of intense research and seeking external validation through a grade. My goal was just not to fail. Spencer and my brother were exploring the life cycle of jellyfish. They proposed that jellyfish were immortal but that no one would ever know because they were always eaten before they could prove their longevity. They explained how they would go about proving this theory and how it would take generations of researchers and several isolated samples of jellyfish. It was an interesting concept, but they didn't have any data to back it up. They would not be in the "A" department either.

Spencer hoped that looking scholarly would help get them a better grade, so he donned a pair of reading glasses. His soft blond locks looked particularly silky today. His weekends on the water were also giving him a head start on a summer tan. I found myself admiring everything about him—even the way he breathed. When Spencer's family business took off, he and his parents had bought a boat. Whenever he wasn't surfing, he was sailing. He had several Boy Scout badges to prove his proficiency as a competent sailor. I imagined myself sailing around the San Diego Bay with him. I knew how to fish—I could be an asset on the boat. I felt a sharp pain as a sudden thought burst into my mind. It wasn't my thought.

"Are you crushing on Spencer?" It was Morgan. He hadn't spoken to me telepathically since Calliope left that afternoon. He walked over to my booth, which was facing theirs. I rubbed my temples. This time it hurt.

"What are you doing? You're not supposed to do that anymore."

Morgan frowned. "I haven't been able to stop. When you're thinking something that has a lot of emotions tied to it, it just flies into my head. Why are you suddenly so obsessed with Spencer?"

"I don't know what you're talking about."

"Oh, okay. Whatever—cut it out."

Spencer left their booth and joined us. I got a weird nervous tingle in my stomach. Morgan raised an eyebrow and shook his head.

"Hey, anyone noticed that Brooke doesn't have a booth?"

I nodded. "I'm pretty surprised. She was almost done with all the research—before this Colin thing."

"Have you even seen her around campus?" Morgan realized that while we were trying to block everything out, we had blocked her out. We did not understand what she and her father were up to. We shared a moment of guilt and grief. We loved her. How could we just not reach out at all? It scared us; we were uncomfortable with everything we were experiencing, but most of all we were selfish. Even if she was crazy and believing everything Colin was feeding her, we knew part of it was true, which made us even worse. Morgan took out his cell phone and called her. As he was dialing, another call came through. It was our dad. Morgan let it go to message. Brooke picked up.

"Hey, cuz. You okay? We good or what?" Morgan blurted into the phone. He nodded several times. "Why aren't you at the science fair? Don't you need this to graduate? . . . I get it. Okay. See you there." I waited anxiously to hear what kind of peace accord they had reached. "So?"

"She's hurt that we didn't believe her or help her. She said she understands now and misses us. She wants to meet at Paradise Point after the science fair." Morgan looked at his phone and noticed a text from our dad. He read the message.

"Mom's in the hospital."

Spencer didn't wait for me to say anything. "Go—you two go. I'll explain to the judges."

We rushed out of the gym and Morgan tried to reach our dad. No response. Luckily, we weren't far from the hospital. Nothing was really that far in this town. If you lived close enough to the coast, you could hop on any freeway and be there in minutes. Normally we would have called

Brooke, but instead we called a car service. We kept messaging our dad and couldn't reach him. I could feel Morgan's worry on top of my worry, and it was exhausting. The limited senses that I could have handled in the past were increasing. It was overwhelming me, but I was fighting it back. I was managing my emotions and his.

We finally connected with my dad. He was waiting out in front of the hospital as the car dropped us off, pacing. He stopped when he saw us. When we reached him, he gave us a big twin bear hug.

"She's okay."

"Well, what happened?" I ventured.

"I took her to see my show today. I wanted to get her thoughts before opening night tomorrow. It's getting a lot of buzz, and I wanted to make sure it was just right. She seemed fine at first, then she just collapsed. Which is a shame, because she only got to see about one-third of the exhibit. I think there will be a lot of press there tomorrow. There is some concern about the eclipse and whether that will keep people away,"

"And what are they saying about Mom? Where is she—can we see her?"

"She's not in her room right now. They have her out for a few more tests. But she has some buildup of heavy metals in her system. Her liver isn't processing them. They will have to do chelation therapy to remove the metals from her system."

Morgan and I shared a thought but say nothing aloud. *"And what medium do you work in and leave shards everywhere—metal!"* Instead, I asked, "Is this what has been causing her illness all along?"

My dad hung his head low. "Sadly, it's not that simple. I guess this is just a new complication, kiddos. It looks like this is just the beginning of some new challenges your mother will be facing." He embraced us and cried. We all cried.

Morgan pulled away, and for a moment questioned Dad's sincerity. "Are you sad for her, or is it something else?"

My dad looked earnestly at him. "I'm sad for all of us. Her illness has really taken a toll on the family. This new piece of her illness might rewrite what could have been our future."

I pushed my father away from me. "I don't know how you can say that it's taken a toll. No more of a toll on our family than your complete focus on your art and lack of focus on us or Mom."

He turned to walk away from me, stunned that I was attacking him. "We all deserve our dreams, Muri." We followed him to the room in silence. We waited and waited in awkward anticipation of her return. Morgan's phone buzzed, and he looked at the message. It was from Spencer. He had let Brooke know that we wouldn't be meeting her at Paradise Point.

My mom looked pale and weak. The nurse who wheeled her in had a kind face but didn't look much older than me. As she helped my mother get out of the chair into the bed, Morgan and I got up to help. She appreciated the extra set of hands, since my mom couldn't support her body weight. The nurse smiled at Morgan. He always got the smiles from the ladies. I leaned in and gave my mother a kiss, and Morgan tucked her in under the covers.

"So, what's going on, Mom?"

The nurse interrupted. "The doctor will be here in a moment to review your final tests. I think they said you might go home."

Morgan pleaded with the nurse. "She doesn't look ready to go anywhere." The nurse smiled. "The doctor should be in soon." She then smiled at my dad and me and walked back into the hall. My mother reached out for Morgan's hand.

"Don't worry. I just had a little setback. They said if they find nothing new in this last set of tests that I could just recover at home and start treatment with my regular doctor."

"Dad said you collapsed!"

"Yes, I was looking at all of your father's beautiful work. I was running my hand along his latest piece, inspired by the mermaid statue in Solvang, and I just don't remember anything else. I woke up here in the hospital."

An older woman in her late fifties entered the room. She extended her hand to my father. "Hello, I'm Dr. Lee. I know you had spoken with Dr. Purcell when your wife first arrived. He's been called away on an emergency." She flipped through my mother's chart. "Even though your case is unusual, it's not untreatable or life-threatening at this point. We can send you home today." Morgan scoffed, "I don't think she should go anywhere. She looks so weak." Dr. Lee walked over to Morgan and placed a hand on his shoulder. "She'll be okay. I promise." She closed the folder. "Just make sure she follows up with her regular physician."

My mother motioned for us to come near her. She was crying. "I'm sorry, my dear hearts. I'm so sorry I have caused you so much worry and trouble. I know you should be at the science fair and your father should be getting ready for his big show tomorrow. I'm so sorry."

We both reached our arms around her and embraced her. I wiped the tears off of her face. "You have nothing to be sorry for!" Morgan echoed my words. "We're just glad that you're okay. We love you!" We looked to my father to chime in and complete our supportive chorus. He didn't move. He didn't say a word. We thought he was resenting her, and we could feel it, and we hated him a little.

"Dad, right?"

He took a deep contemplative breath. "Yes, of course. Not your fault." The minutes crept along as we waited for the discharge papers. We just wanted to send my father away. I could feel the heat in Morgan's belly coming from his anger. He wanted Dad to open his eyes and be someone different. Someone who cared more than he did. Someone who loved our mother the way she deserved to be loved and cherished. Why did his dreams matter? Who was he anyway, other than the guy whose genes came with a curse? As Morgan and I shared these thoughts, we froze as Nohea and Brooke walked through the hospital room door carrying a bouquet. Now my father got to his feet.

"What are you guys doing here?"

My mother raised her voice. "Mitchell. I called them." Nohea looked surprised by this comment. We could also tell from Brooke's face that this was a lie. Our mother—ever the peacemaker.

"I'm glad you came."

Nohea came to my mother's bedside. Brooke placed the flowers on a nearby table and then sat on the other side of my mother's bed. Tears streamed down Brooke's face, but she didn't seem like she was crying. The rest of her body was still. Just the tears. She took a deep cleansing breath through her nose.

"Are you okay?"

My mother patted her hand. "I will be."

My uncle adjusted my mother's pillow. My father stood close by, feeling threatened in his comforting territory.

"When can you go home?"

My dad answered for her. "She's coming home tonight."

Just then, the fresh-faced nurse came in with her release papers and care plan.

"Will there be someone at home with her? She shouldn't be alone for the next 24 hours in case her condition changes. If it does, bring her to the emergency room immediately."

Morgan and I listened intently. "Yes—no problem, we'll be with her."

My dad scratched his head awkwardly and spoke into the air, as if no one might be listening.

"I have my show tomorrow. I'll be gone most of the day and night."

I frowned. "Of course you will."

Morgan looked at the nurse. "We will be with her."

My uncle spoke up. "Yes, we will be with her. While you kids are in school, I will stay with your mom. No need to worry. We're family."

My father stepped in. "No, we'll figure it out."

Brooke was oddly silent, weighted down by something more than our disagreement. I could sense her feelings. She was feeling guilty about something. Maybe for fighting with us? She also felt hopeful. Could I read everyone's feelings now? Morgan answered this question silently.

"I can feel it too. She's up to something."

Before the kiss with Colin, Brooke and I were sisters. We fell into the perfect big sister/little sister dynamic. The beauty of our relationship was that we were better than sisters. Cousins could share all the common things like family stories and live the "blood is thicker than water" mantra. It was us first and everyone else second. Yet, the perk of not being sisters was that we didn't have to share the important stuff like parents, a room, or any of our stuff. There was no fighting for resources—so it was easy to be closer than sisters. No competition of any kind. Just pure love and support. Within a few odd moments our rock-solid bond had crumbled. I wondered if we would ever get it back. I hoped for the possibility. I not only loved her, there was a bit of hero worship. She was strong and brave even after losing her mother. She occupied a space in reality that I wished I could inhabit. I spent most of my time in the past and future, worried about what it all meant and what would happen next. The present moment was hers. The future was mine, and it worried me.

We gathered my mother's things together and wheeled her out of the hospital. My dad, hesitant to leave us, rushed to go find the car, leaving us with Nohea and Brooke. Brooke suddenly embraced me. At first I stiffened in the hug, feeling slightly violated, but then I could feel the apology in this hug and I gave in to it. Her energy was strong and warm, filled with love, but as she pulled out of the hug, I could feel the guilt as if it were a bee stinging me. Even after she let me go, my skin reverberated with it. My stomach flipped, and I ran to the corner to vomit. Brooke looked confused. Morgan also felt it. He covered for me.

"That's how emotionally constipated she is. Hug her and she

vomits."

My mother disapproved of Morgan heckling me and motioned to Nohea to wheel her over to me. She rubbed my back, ever the loving and nurturing mother. I felt a rage fill up in the air. I felt Brooke's guilt turning into rage.

"Muri—I hope you're not getting sick."

I straightened up and caught Brooke's hot gaze. "No, I think it was just the stress and lunch."

My dad finally arrived with the car and we went our separate ways. In the back of the car, Morgan quietly yet not telepathically asked about Brooke. *"What was her deal? Something is up."*

We shared a moment of pure worry and foreboding. *"I don't know—but I don't trust her. She's not the same anymore."*

"We need to figure out what's up with her and why she feels so guilty."

Morgan read my thoughts and shook his head. *"No. I don't want to start that again."*

"I think we have to."

Back at the house, we all tucked my mother into bed. My dad stepped out quietly to talk about tomorrow's plan.

"We know, Dad. You won't be here."

"I think you two should skip school tomorrow and stay home with your mother."

"What about Uncle Nohea?"

"If I can't be here, then I want you guys to be here for your mother."

"Are you sure you can't be here, or do you just not want to be here?"

"Come on—you know this is a big deal. After tomorrow I can be here more. It will get better. I know you think I don't care about your mother enough, but you're wrong. I love her very much."

I sneered a bit and shrugged. "Okay. I'm fine with taking the day off."

Morgan shook his head. "I'm here after school but I have a test tomorrow. I'll skip out after that."

My dad agreed that would work and headed back into the room with my mother. We could hear the cooking show already playing.

"Hey, I'm calling Calliope."

"I don't think we should."

"I will try it solo if I have to. Since we're talking about her, you know, she's already here...."

We quietly entered my bedroom, and I took the pearl comb out of the drawer. We put our hands on it together, and we could see Calliope again.

"Hello, Luteys."

"Calliope, what is going on with our cousin Brooke?"

"Your cousin is filled with anger about the loss of her mother. She's making plans to get her back from the sea."

"You said that's not possible."

"It's not."

"What's her plan? Do you think if we have her see you, we can change her mind?"

"She's already seen me."

Morgan dropped to the floor and sat down. "Why are you messing with us? Brooke has known all along? No wonder she's so mad at us."

I pulled out my notebook and reviewed my notes. "Why didn't you tell us she could call you?"

Calliope got very close to the two of us and whispered. "She can't. Colin calls me every day. The only thing that keeps me from his side is when you call me. By the way. Thank you for that."

I flipped through the pages of my notebook once again. I had added my research over the past few days. "I don't understand. Is Colin also a Lutey or a Pellar?" I had learned the name of the other branch of our family that shared the Lutey bloodline and curse.

"No, he is nephilim."

"What? Why does he look normal? What does he want?"

"I'm bound by an oath and cannot say. But I will say that I'm sorry that I can't tell you, and I will help in any way that I am able."

Morgan pulled out his phone. He sent Brooke a message.

"We know what you're up to. Let's talk."

She responded. "Meet me at Paradise Point. Bring the comb."

We peeked in on my parents. Morgan called Spencer with his newly minted driver's license for a ride. We piled into his dad's old VW bus—his new ride. We were headed for the quaint little part of the bay known as Paradise Point Resort. My brother let me sit up front. Morgan briefly touched my hand in reassurance as I got into the van. It startled me, but I was grateful for it.

"How's your mom?"

"I think she's okay."

"What's the deal now? Why are we meeting Brooke?" Morgan pointed to a turn in the road.

"This is the way to our family spot. She's got some crazy ideas that we need to help get straightened out."

Even though we had lived in San Diego our entire lives, there were still places that filled our imaginations and hearts with magic. Every summer and every winter, we packed a picnic, picked out a spot, and settled into paradise. Tourists and locals loved this place. They could rent a little cottage, bring jet-skis, rent sailboats or paddle boards, or just go for a swim. The beaches that surrounded the bay were all public access, but most people didn't know that, so it was never too crowded. Some people liked to sit in cafés and people-watch, but our family did it from here. Sometimes we were voting on which college rowing group had the best form or which boozy pontoon boaters were from out of town. As tweens, we developed a game called "tourist or local." I based my guesses on the level of their sunburn.

If it was available, we set up on the patch of sand in front of the presidential residence. This was basically the nicest and largest cottage on the property with the best and most secluded view (although I'm sure no president ever stayed there). It never pleased the guests of that room when we set up on what they thought was their private stretch of beach. Fortunately for us, the price was so steep that few guests could afford it, so it felt like our private beach. Brooke and her family had joined us many times. Tonight I wasn't excited to see her on our sand.

Spencer parked his van at the edge of the cottage cluster. He didn't want to be towed for taking a guest's space. We told him it never happened, but he wasn't about to lose the car he'd been waiting years to drive. I could see Brooke next to the twin palm trees that we stood in front of for every holiday card picture. She was alone. That was a good sign. I had hope. I could sense that Morgan didn't. He hopped out of the car and hurried toward her. Spencer and I tried to get out and catch up. He was inches from Brooke's face.

"Don't shut us out, Brooke. We are all dealing with this weird new reality."

She backed up a step, giving herself physical and emotional space from Morgan. His intensity radiated like waves of heat. "Did you bring the comb?" I held it out for her to see it. Her shoulders relaxed. Relieved, she picked a spot on the sand and sat down.

"Why did you want me to bring it?"

"I needed to know that you really had it and that I could trust you."

"You can trust us, Brooke. It's always been us with you. We love you!" Spencer wasn't understanding the family reunion.

"I don't get what's going on? Why are we here?"

"May I hold the comb?" I started to put it in her hand, but Spencer snatched it from me. He motioned to a figure off in the distance.

"Is that Colin?" Brooke reached for the comb. Spencer blocked her, but Brooke, being nimble and able to ride the waves and navigate the rocks, outmaneuvered him. She grabbed the comb. Colin now stood next to her, and we could no longer move. Calliope flanked Brooke on the other side. Brooke stepped closer to me.

"Tomorrow I will have my mother back."

"And how exactly is that going to work? It's not possible. She's gone."

Colin brought out the book we had seen in the library of the mythological creatures. "She will do an exchange. She will return someone to the sea for her mother."

Morgan struggled to break free from whatever was immobilizing him. He looked at Calliope. She was trying to communicate with him, but he couldn't hear.

"Who. Who are you returning to the sea?" Brooke looked at me with guilt and disdain.

"Your mother."

Morgan sent a telepathic message to me: *Let's focus on Spencer— maybe we can free him and he can get help.* With that thought, Colin waved his hand and Spencer fell to the ground.

"I'm privy to your thoughts, my boy."

"Why my mother? She's ill. Are you trying to kill her?"

"We're trying to set her free."

Then something happened that no nephilim or human could have expected: the power in a teenage girl with a double curse or gift. Calliope had experienced a piece of my fear, but no one had experienced a full explosion of rage, fear, panic, and a meltdown I had been preparing for my whole life. This was the scream of a banshee. I could feel it rising and rising as the anger grew with the threat on my mother. The most pure and wonderful person who had raised me with compassion and grace no matter what I put her through. I spent my long days containing the weird, ever-present twinge under my skin that might result in a tic or an overemotional moment. All of that pent-up anxiety released in this moment. I was free to move.

Colin kneeled on the ground, covering his ears. Brooke fell and lay unconscious. Morgan looked stunned by my sonic boom, but he too was free. The only creature unfazed was Calliope. She smiled as I continued to scream. As I looked around, I didn't realize that I was still making a sound. The windows shook in the nearby presidential suite. No human in my vicinity was conscious. In the bay, several sea lions appeared. They swam to the shoreline and began their own chorus. I couldn't tell if they were joining me or asking me to shut up. Calliope touched my arm and brought my attention back to the present moment.

"You and your brother need to hide your mother until after the total solar eclipse tomorrow."

Morgan tugged at Spencer's motionless body and brought him to his feet. We supported his body weight and moved toward the van. I stopped screaming, and Colin was quickly on his feet and blocking our way. I didn't have any scream left in me, but I stood my ground. The sea lions scattered and disappeared into the bay. Morgan tried to drag Spencer to the van on his own but couldn't, so he put him down and stood by my side.

"Valiant effort. You may depart. But this will happen. There is nothing that can stop it," Colin smirked.

"Leave our mother alone. Whatever it is you want to happen, it can't happen. Calliope told us that Brooke's mother can't come back. And even if she could, we're not about to trade our mother for hers."

"So selfish, Lutey. Your kind always professes to be helpers, but you are always just helping yourselves."

"What's your grudge against us, nephilim?"

"No grudge. I have one mission to accomplish. I've been waiting for tomorrow's eclipse. I won't wait for the next one."

Colin dismissed us. "Go, there is nothing you can do. Enjoy your last night with your mother."

I wished that I had another blast in me that could decimate his smug face, but I had nothing. They had our comb, and I felt like I was losing my voice completely. I tried to call out to Morgan, and I couldn't.

Calliope called out to me instead. "Go, child. Go."

Colin turned and walked toward Brooke and helped her up. Morgan, Spencer, and I reached the van and drove home in a daze. No one spoke until Spencer broke the silence.

"So those nut jobs are going to try and toss your mother into the ocean tomorrow during the eclipse?"

"I wasn't sure how much of that you got. But that's what it looks like. So we have to figure something out. Muri—any ideas?"

I tried to speak and couldn't. I motioned to my throat and cried. Luckily, my brother could read my thoughts.

"The RV?"

"What about the RV?"

"We could hijack Mom for the day."

Spencer shook his head. "My dad already loaned it to my cousin. She took it yesterday to Idaho to see the eclipse with her friends. I guess she'll be in the path of totality."

"What the heck is that?"

"Where she's staying it will be completely blacked out when the moon passes in front of the sun."

"What about where we are?" I thought.

Morgan asked for me. "What about here?"

"It will look like the moon took a bite out of the sun."

Spencer dropped us off with no plan in place except that he would return in the morning before the eclipse and that we would take my mom somewhere. There wouldn't be much time, since the eclipse would start at about nine in the morning.

Morgan and I quietly packed up for the unknown. Maybe we would take her back to Solvang or go all the way to the Redwoods. I packed all of her favorite foods, pain medicine, and loaded all of her favorite baking shows on my tablet. If we had to be gone forever, I would be prepared. I could feel Morgan's uncertainty and guilt.

"What are you thinking?" My voice was gone.

"What about Dad? I think we need to just tell him. We need his help. We can't just take Mom somewhere the day of his big show."

I agreed, so we walked quietly to my parents' room and urged my father to come out to talk with us. He saw our bags.

"Aren't you guys a little too old to run away from home?" He chuckled.

"I need you to have an open mind. There is crazy stuff going down with Brooke, Colin, and her dad. They think if they take Mom and dump her in the ocean that they'll get Aunt Mallory back."

My father sat down on the couch. "Nohea said he had some idea involving your mother. I didn't realize it was that insane."

"You knew?"

"Well, I knew he thought your mother could help him somehow. So I threatened him and told him I would call the police. I guess that's my next step. That's why I didn't want any help from him."

"I don't think the police will do anything to stop them. They won't believe us."

"Let me get through my show tomorrow, then we'll deal with this."

I started waving my hands in the air. I could eke out a whisper. "It will be too late."

My father looked frustrated and tired. "What was the plan with the bags?"

"We're going to take Mom away for a while."

"Just go to bed, guys. You have school. I have my show. I can contact the police soon enough. I'll talk to them once more. Maybe they'll come to their senses. I understand what grief can do to you. I just can't deal with this right now. Just go to bed."

So Morgan and I pretended to go to bed, with the understanding that we would continue with our plan. When the sun rose before the moon could pass it and eclipse, we would take our mother far away from any of them. We had our eclipse glasses from school, and nothing would get in the way of protecting our mother—not even the moon. We packed and plotted, waiting for our father to fall asleep, but then I dozed off.

When I woke up, Morgan was standing over me, distraught. "We overslept!"

"How is that possible?" My voice was back. He pulled open my curtains and revealed the half-light and orange hazy sky. I leapt out of bed and ran to my mother's room. Morgan was a pace behind me. He hadn't thought to check on my mother first. Her bed was empty. I raced through the house, calling to her.

"Mom! Mom! Dad, are you home?" I looked out the window—no car. There was a note on the kitchen counter from our dad, discovered by Morgan. It just read: "Gone to work. Take care of your mother. We'll deal with the other stuff later. Love you guys. Dad."

"Call Spencer. Why didn't he wake us?"

There was a pounding on the door. It was Spencer. "I overslept. Can we still get your mom outta here? I think I can drive if I don't look directly at the sun. Oh, and I can use the eclipse glasses." I put my shoes on and threw a hoodie over my pajamas.

"She's gone already!"

Morgan grabbed our "go" bags.

"Paradise Point. I know that's where they are. I can feel it."

I called my dad and left him a frantic message. We raced to the San Diego Bay, making sure not to look directly at the sun. None of us were wearing our glasses. We were in too much of a rush to remember that we had them. We pulled into the resort. Tourists were lined up with their eclipse glasses watching the sky—no one was watching the water, except us. Brooke and Colin were on a pontoon boat in the center of the bay. Nohea was in a small motorboat with my mother, approaching the pontoon slowly.

"How are we going to reach them?"

Morgan noticed a jet-ski sitting near the edge of the beach. The rider had gotten off to experience the eclipse. He was apparently un-aware of eclipse protocol and was looking directly at the sun. I re-membered my glasses and reminded the boys. The jet-ski would fit only two. Morgan and I hopped on, and Spencer ran interference in case the owner noticed that we had borrowed it. We reached the boat as Nohea was loading my mother onto it. We thought he was going to throw her overboard, but we saw him carefully lifting her onboard. They saw us coming but didn't change anything. The boat was just parked, waiting in the middle of the bay for its cargo. We were unsure of what to do when we got to the boat. Could we leap on board? Morgan steadied the jet-ski and tried to get close enough. He turned the engine off, and we drifted near the boat. We jumped into the water and swam to the edge of the pontoon boat. When we reached the vessel, Nohea and Brooke had their hands held out to the water to help us aboard.

"Take our hands."

"Why?"

Morgan climbed on the boat without their help, but I continued to struggle. Brooke reached deeper into the water and grabbed a bit of my hoodie. She and her father pulled me aboard. Morgan was behind them, ready to push them into the water, but Colin appeared with my mother, who looked like she was in a trance.

"Don't." I was shivering from the cold water. "Stop this craziness. You can't bring Aunt Mallory back! I've seen her—she's dead. She's not coming back."

Brooke fumed. "I told you, Dad. We'd have to do this without them. There's no point telling them the truth about their mother. They'd never help us."

"What truth?" I grabbed her and shook her. Brooke stood solidly. Morgan was by my mother's side, trying to stay as close to her as pos-sible. Colin waved his hand, and I lost my footing, falling to the floor of the boat.

Nohea tried to plead with everyone. "From the beginning I wanted everyone to be honest. Let's be honest. Your mother is very sick. She is not meant to be on dry land for so long or to be so close to metal elements. We are returning her to her home and getting your Aunt Mallory. I believe we are doing what is right."

Morgan and I could not deny that our mother was ill. We also knew that her recent diagnosis mentioned a buildup of metal in her blood, which we assumed had to do with my father's artwork or the bad city water. The rest was crazy. She was not a Lutey. She was not a water person. She was just a poor sick woman with insane relatives. Nohea pleaded with Colin.

"Let them say goodbye to their mother. My child didn't have that luxury. Please."

Colin waved a hand over my mother's face, and she was there again. She saw us and knew us. Colin allowed us to embrace her. She looked around, confused.

"Where are we?"

Nohea was quick with the answer. "We're watching the eclipse from a pontoon boat. Remember?"

She nodded as if she vaguely remembered. "Yes, okay. I remember."

I wrapped my arms around my mother. "I love you, Mom. Thank you for everything you have ever done for me. Thank you for always believing in me."

She stroked my hair as she always did. As my tears fell on her skin, she suddenly had a bright look of awareness. Morgan wrapped his arms around both of us and his tears also touched her skin. I could feel the warm glow of our love fill all of us. She wiped his tears from his face.

She whispered softly, "Soon I may not know you, but I will always love you."

Colin handed Brooke a sheet of old parchment paper and reclaimed his hold on my mother. Brooke placed the pearl comb in my mother's hair. Colin pushed us to the side with simply a finger. He was getting stronger as the moon was covering the sun completely. "It's time."

Brooke read aloud: "Je vous commande de retourner à la mer. Mwen kòmande ou pou retounen nan lanmè. I command you to return to the sea!"

My mother moved away from Colin. Morgan and I tried to reach her but were held in place by some unseen force. My mother walked to the edge of the boat. The sky was black. She took her hair out of her bun, and the dark silky curls flowed in the wind. Only the pearl comb kept them out of her face. She stood on the edge of the boat and dove in, so easy and smooth with barely a ripple to the water surface. Morgan and I could move, but not past the edge of the boat where we would have wanted to dive in after her. I shrieked but couldn't summon my powerful scream. Brooke and Nohea embraced each other and looked anxiously over the side.

"When will my mother appear?"

Colin laughed. "Your mother won't be returning."

My cousin and uncle looked sick. Nohea lunged at Colin. Colin laughed even harder.

"We had a deal."

"Yes, we had a deal. We would return Lorelei to the sea and break the Lutey curse. We will take no more Luteys to the sea, and no Lutey will ever have any power over a mermaid or other creature again for good or evil. It's done."

Brooke was hysterical. Morgan and I watched it unfold like we weren't there, in shock over watching our mother dive into the bay. I thought about Calliope and wondered where she was. Morgan pushed a thought into my brain.

"I can still hear your thoughts! Where is Calliope?" We thought and thought about Calliope, and suddenly she was in our presence. She was not alone. She was with two other sirens. Colin seemed startled by their appearance.

"I didn't call you."

"No—they did." Calliope looked in our direction and smiled. Our powers seemed to get stronger, not weaker. The pontoon boat rocked. The water swirled around us. High walls of water. Sea lions, dolphins, seals, and all kinds of fish were swimming around the boat. Then we saw her—my mother. My mother, the mermaid.

Chapter 8

The eclipse was at its most intense moment. The sky was dark, and the water reflected the muddled colors of the moon and sun meeting in the middle. My mother was halfway out of the water. Her long black hair glistened in the strange light. Her eyes were black like a seal's—no visible white—and her alabaster skin shimmered and subtly shifted colors as we saw the rest of her mermaid body. Her hips were covered with shiny iridescent scales of purple, rose, and aquamarine. She rose out of the water, and her wild hair was caught in the wind. She looked at us, and we rushed to the side of the boat and called out to her.

"Mom, Mom. Mom." She stared through us, leapt high into the air, and dove deep. Her fin had flecks of yellow and orange intermingled with purple hues, a striking contrast to the aquamarine and rose scales just above the base of her tail. Her fin hit the water and created a wave that entered the boat, and then the water was still. Brooke was by our side, watching my mother dive away from us. One of Calliope's siren friends spoke. She had golden curls that framed her angelic face. Even her wings were more fairy- or angel-like than bird-like.

"Child. She doesn't know you now. She is wild. The Sea has her."

I turned and started shaking Brooke. "Are you happy now? Neither of us has a mother now!" Colin turned to the sirens.

"Go away. Our business is done." They didn't move.

"It's not done. There is no reason they need to suffer."

Brooke pleaded, "Can you return my mother? I mean our mothers?"

Calliope shook her head.

"Muriel told you the truth. Your mother has died. She is no longer part of this mortal coil. He needed you, a person of Lutey blood, to free Lorelei from this ancient, misunderstood curse."

The moon passed the sun and was free to shine again. The water reflected its brilliance. An enormous sea turtle like the one from my dream surfaced. They didn't normally enter the bay. They lived safely off in the distance, away from the naval ships and kayakers. The stillness on the bay was ending. Boats started up, and motors rippled the water.

"I don't understand." Morgan looked at the angelic siren and spoke softly to her. "What has happened here? This curse turned my mother into a mermaid?"

"Long ago, as a baby, your mother, who has always been a mermaid, was caught in a net near a place called Victoria. Her mother searched and searched for her and was seen by your kind several times in the area and forced to stop looking. It is unknown who took her from the net. Colin is one of many who search for our lost ones and bring them home."

"How would we never have known she was a mermaid—and what's the connection with the Luteys?"

"Somehow she became a captive to the Luteys' will and their curse, or she may have discovered her identity on her own." Calliope muttered. "They foretold it. A mermaid of great power would break the last bond or curse humankind had over the nephilim."

Colin smiled. "It is the beginning of our time again. God will not be disappointed in his creations again."

"How can I find my mother?"

My uncle Nohea rose to his feet. The sirens and Colin vanished.

"Where are we?" He rubbed his head.

"Don't talk to me! You're the reason my mother is gone!" I shoved him, trying to knock him overboard. My full weight and force didn't move him. He looked around quickly and called out. "Mallory? Mallory?"

Brooke reached out to her father. "She's not here, Dad. It was a trick."

Suddenly a fine sea mist engulfed us. Then there was a change in both of their faces. They started speaking slowly and there was a zombie quality to their speech. My uncle spoke first.

"It's no one's fault. You both lost your mothers to the sea. It's a tragedy—but no one's fault."

Brooke then responded, or more like chanted. "No one's fault."

"What are you talking about? You're definitely to blame here!" Morgan stood toe to toe with our much bigger uncle. My uncle got his bearings and saw where we were. He noticed the eclipse glasses but was still dazed. He took the helm of the pontoon boat and drove us toward the shore. The jet-ski had long since floated away.

"I wish I could have stopped your Aunt Mallory and your mother from going out that day, but none of us could have known that it would have ended in tragedy. We're all healing." Brooke sidled up to her father, and he put her arm around her.

Morgan looked at me, questioning what was happening. "Brooke, when was the last time you saw our mother?"

"When we all did. Before she and my mother went out on the boat."

"So you didn't see my mother today?" Morgan looked suspiciously at Brooke.

Brooke and her father looked at each other, puzzled. "Of course not."

We reached the shore, where Spencer was waiting for us anxiously. He saw that we were alone with Brooke and Nohea and was cautious about speaking. He looked to Morgan for a cue.

"Hey, what's up?"

Morgan and I hopped off of the boat quickly. We shared thoughts easily with rapid-fire communication.

"Say nothing of substance!" I pushed this thought into Morgan's mind. I was privy to his thoughts now—not just his emotions. We were connected on a deeper level than ever before.

Morgan directed his comment to Spencer. "We saw the eclipse and now we need a ride to our dad's show." I pushed a thought into Morgan's mind. *"We have to go after mom. We have to find her!"* I occupied a corner of Morgan's mind with ease.

"We need to get Spencer alone. To see if he's still with us!" He responded to me without words. Spencer was hesitant but went with it.

"Okay, um. Sure. Let's get going."

Nohea spoke up. "Guys, I'm not sure what's going on with you— but we can take you to your father's show and discuss all of this more."

"No, we're good. Uh, we'll see you there."

"We have to return the boat, but we won't be too far behind," Nohea reassured us. Brooke still had a slight zombie quality to her. They both seemed like they were inhabiting their bodies from a distance. Another sea turtle surfaced, and I saw it out of the corner of my eye.

Once we were clear of Brooke and Nohea, Morgan quizzed Spencer. "Do you know why we're here?"

"To save your mom from the clutches of the evil rainbow researcher Colin and your cousin."

Morgan sighed with relief and patted Spencer on the back. "Yes, for a moment I wasn't sure what you would know. Brooke and Nohea are acting like they have no memory of our little boat trip of disaster."

"Where's your mom?"

"Well, that's a tough one. She dove overboard." I started hyperventilating and crying while trying to explain to Spencer. "Her eyes, her eyes went dark. Her face, it was different. She didn't know us." I fell to the ground and angrily started throwing sand and rocks at the water and screamed, "Mom."

I saw the turtle by the edge of the bay. "I'm going after her."

Morgan put his arm around me, trying to soothe me. He was lost and hazy. His mind was filled with grief and fear. "Where would you even look?"

I pointed toward the turtle. "I'm going with him."

"How?"

"Trust me. I think he will take me to her."

"You don't surf and don't really like nature—and you're heading off on a turtle?"

Spencer was concerned. Morgan knew I thought it was what I needed to do. He was just as desperate as I was, so he didn't stop me. "I'll get to Dad before Nohea and let him know what happened so he can help!"

The boys watched me quietly approach the sea turtle. It motioned to me—as if telling me to climb on board. The turtle gently entered the water past the edge of the sandy shelf into the deep water. I waded in behind him and then put my hands on the side of his shell like he was a boogie board. He glided deeper into the bay, making sure my head stayed above the salty sea water. He swam north out of the inlet into the deep waters. The water was icy cold, and my nerves were frayed. His shell was oddly slimy and warm. He looked back at me every few moments, checking on me. I felt things swim by my feet and seaweed got caught around my ankles. I was not feeling at home in the water. The image of my mother and her dark, almost glowing eyes frightened me. Was she still my mother? Was I truly her daughter—how could any of this be real? The water stung my eyes as little sprays moved up the sides of the turtle's shell. A companion turtle swam to the other side of me, creating a smoother current for me to be in the flow. Waves crashed over us. We entered a tube and glided, enclosed and protected by the waves—protected from the real depths of the sea.

I recognized the coastline—we were almost to La Jolla. We were entering an area that I'd known my whole life, La Jolla Cove. The area was usually spattered with people scuba diving, snorkeling, ocean swimming, and kayaking, but today, because of the eclipse, all I saw were garibaldi, the super-bright orange fish that called this place home. The sea cliffs buffered the high surf. The turtles guided me through the calm waters east toward the La Jolla Sea Caves. The caves—they must be our destination. I noticed the garibaldi were no longer our only companions. There were sea lions inhabiting the area. They sprawled out on the rocks. Some sunned themselves; others dove in and out of the water, splashing. There were hundreds taking up every inch of free rock space. When they saw me, they took notice. A few swam in near me, baring their teeth and barking or grunting. The panic was rising inside my body. My wet clothes were heavy and dragging me down. Things had attached themselves to me along the way. I was too scared to see what was clinging to my shirt and pants. My thoughts raced: *I'm swimming toward the sea coves with 500-pound bull sea lions establishing their territory inches from my face.* The turtles kept swimming, unfettered.

What was my plan? Well, first off not to drown—say an Our Father prayer and ask them nicely to leave me alone. "Our Father, who art in heaven, hallowed be thy Name, thy kingdom come, thy will be done, on earth as it is in heaven—please sea lions, leave me alone." With that the sea lions quieted, stopped swimming, and turned back toward their rocks. The turtles looked at me and it seemed like they were smiling. They listened. Yet more sea lions entered the water. They growled and grunted, and dozens slid from their rocks into the water. With each entry I felt more and more buoyant, as if we were all ice cubes in a glass of water. I was floating closer to the surface. They were creating some type of barrier behind me. The turtle turned suddenly and shook me loose. I was bobbing unassisted in the water. I couldn't have gone under if I had tried. I felt the eyes of the creatures on me. What now? Screaming was definitely an option, but I'm not sure what the point would have been because no one was doing anything but looking and maybe waiting. Were they waiting for me to speak again?

Then I realized it wasn't me they were waiting for. I saw the glimmer of a magical orange-tinged fin; the garibaldi camouflaged the ends of the purple and rose-hued scales. She was swimming past me, next to me, then in front of me. She emerged from the water within reach. I recognized her as my mother, but also as someone I had never seen before. Someone who was a stranger to me. The water and my blood grew cold. I could barely feel my hands in the water. Then my brain buzzed as if she were tapping at the entrance to my mind. Her eyes flickered with a moment of knowing. I could hear her in my heart. *"Who are you? Do I know you?"* Then she opened her mouth and made sounds I only recognized as a dolphin's call—squeaks and clicks. She was frustrated by her inability to speak words and tried again, but I heard her inside my mind. *"Who are you? Do I know you?"* She rose up high on her tail in confusion.

"You are my mother! I am your daughter. You know me!"

She paused for a moment. I made it through to her mind—she knew me. Then I could see the fear on her face. She looked at me and then at our surroundings. She had a flash of our old life and was frightened by what she had become. I could hear her thoughts. *"Is my name Lorelei? Am I your mother?"*

A violent wave broke through the line of sea lions. A thunderous, overwhelming chorus of clicks and squeaks infiltrated the moment. My mother's eyes went black and primal. She answered with her own pained sounds and they overtook us. Dolphins. A pod of dolphins leaped over the sea lions. The cove wasn't equipped to handle this tumultuous gathering of sea life. The waves lapped up hard and high against the cliffs. The saltwater sprayed in my eyes and nose. I tried to keep my mouth closed, to keep the water out. The sea lions tried to circle us and create a protective barrier, but nothing stopped the movement of the dolphins.

They slapped the water with their tails, squeaked, and bullied the regular cove inhabitants. My mother dove underwater and away from me. I reached out and swam as fast as I could toward her. My hands grasped at the wisps on her fin. The powerful mermaid kick of her tail took her quickly away and left me swirling in its wake. I needed air and broke free of the water to the surface. My turtle friends swam toward me as I struggled. My eyes were cloudy and stinging from the cold salty water, but I could see a man swimming among the dolphins. His hair was sun-bleached, long, and wavy, and he wasn't wearing a rash guard or wetsuit. He held on to the dorsal fin of a nearby dolphin and wrapped a long piece of seaweed like a harness around it. He dove into the water, and I could see the rest of his body covered in shimmering green-blue scales and an almost black tail fin. When he re-emerged, he had my mother caught in his arms. She struggled as he wrapped a part of the seaweed around her waist and her hand. She, too, was now wearing a gentle harness. The two sea creatures bound together.

Another dolphin arrived, and the merman tied the end of the seaweed to its dorsal fin, trapping my mother between the two dolphins. The turtles slid under my arms and positioned me between them, much like my mother betwixt the cetaceans. The merman raised his body high out of the water and blew a small conch shell, and before I could blink, all the dolphins dove silently beneath the surface and were gone. The ripples in the water showed their movement, heading out of the cove. The harnessed mammals and my mother were gone as well. I pushed away from the turtles and swam toward the current. The merman looked back at me for a brief moment but then dove deep. The water became still.

With that last look, all my strength left me. I noticed a weird clanking sound...I soon determined it was my teeth chattering. I was losing my ability to move. The sea lions swam back to their rocks. The sea turtles repositioned themselves and nudged my body into the sea caves. I clung to the rocks and made my way to an area the sea lions must have called home—since they had stained it with their urine and poop. But I didn't have a choice—this was my refuge. My body and mind were giving up on me. The turtles swam away. A seagull gawked at me from a high perch. I closed my eyes to rest, hoping that it would be all right when I woke.

I was having the dream. The one where oysters attached to my feet. I felt the pinching and opened my eyes. A lovely girl with dark skin and wavy reddish-blonde hair was picking seaweed and sand crabs from my legs and toes. She had beautiful tan and brown feathers on her lower torso, and I noticed her matching wings closed and attached to her back. Her legs were like Calliope's—like a bird's, with talons—but her hands were very human. She hummed a soft tune that calmed and warmed me. She leaned over me and saw me waking. Her smile filled me with peace. I took a deep breath through my nose and smiled back. Part of my brain was still dreaming, and the other part realized that I was in the La Jolla sea caves and that my mother... I didn't know.

"Hello," she ventured.

My eyes were sore from the salt water and crying. I rubbed them gently to get a better look at her. She helped me sit up. My body was heavy, and my clothes were wet. She returned to her humming, and as she touched me my body felt lighter and warmer. I positioned myself against the rock of the sea cave to help support me. I finally had my voice: "Hello."

She sat next to me, and I was not afraid. She motioned to me and opened one of her wings, like she wanted to wrap it around me, warming the cool rock wall behind me. "May I?"

I nodded in agreement. Her warm, soft feathers cradled me, and her warmth filled me up. "Who are you?"

I knew that she was a siren, but I didn't remember her from the pontoon boat.

"I am Melpomene."

"I'm Muriel."

I could tell she already knew this, but she politely continued. "Nice to meet you. Are you feeling any better?"

"Uh, yes. I guess so."

"Do you think you can call your brother to retrieve you?"

I looked around the cave in wonder. I realized that she was a supernatural creature, but even she had to realize that my cell phone didn't make the journey. "I don't have a phone."

She smiled sweetly. There was no mocking in her tone, only kindness. "You could try with your heart and your thoughts. He already knows that he needs to find you. He just doesn't know where to look."

"I think that brain thing only works when we're together. In the same space."

"Try."

I took another deep breath and looked around the cave and thought about how I got here. Thinking about it made me shiver and cry. Melpomene hummed softly to comfort me. I relaxed and had a deep knowing that Morgan was on his way.

"Mel ... Meloponem ... I'm sorry I don't remember how to say your name."

She interrupted me. "You may call me Mel if that's easier."

I nodded in appreciation and started again. "Mel, I think it worked. I feel like he's on his way."

She patted my hand gently. "This is good."

I realized that it didn't seem weird at all that I was sitting next to a feathered, talking half-human of some sort. My reality had forever shifted.

"I don't understand what's happening. Do you know that these dolphins and a merperson took my mother?"

She retracted her wing and scooted slightly away from me so she could look at my face. She caressed my cheek for a moment. She could feel my anxiousness rising. She hummed a little to keep me calm before she spoke.

"Yes, I know. Your mother is a wild mermaid now. She is being taken to her home with her tribe. They will help her and teach her. She must be very frightened now, but it will be better soon."

"How is she a mermaid? How is this possible?"

Melpomene reached into her feathers around her waist. I looked closer. She had feathers, but she also was clothed in blue peacock feathers woven together. She pulled out a thin emerald, pearl, and seashell–encrusted oval mirror.

"Show me Lorelei." A beautiful mermaid with long golden curly hair sat sunning herself on a rock. Her skin had a peaches and cream quality to it, and her tail had shimmering scales of yellow and green. She would blend in nicely with seaweed or light sea grasses. Her hair was adorned with a crown of red coral and pearls that glimmered between the curls. She cradled a blanket of bright green eelgrass, a dark-haired baby swaddled within it. The image faded from the mirror.

"Is that it? How does that help me? I need to know everything." Melpomene ran her hand in front of the mirror, but nothing else happened. "I'm sorry, Muriel. We are not omniscient beings. We only know what we know and what it allows us to see."

"Well, tell me what you know."

"Much of what I know I was told by Colin when he enlisted us to help him. We knew some of it seemed strange, but our job is to help your kind. They took your mother as a baby from the sea before she had any true knowledge of who she was. They raised her in your human world and somehow she fell under the power of the Lutey clan and became truly lost. She would have died if not returned to the sea. Now she is a feral creature that must learn the ways of the sea and her people."

"What about us, her children? We must find her!"

"You must be found first." With this, Mel, as I would call her forever, disappeared. I called out to her, and then I called out to Calliope, but no one appeared except a curious sea lion. He grunted and barked at me to move along and get off of his rock. I was still getting my bearings as the sea lion got closer and closer. I finally had a complete awareness of where I was. I was in one of the seven sister caves in La Jolla. I knew all about this place, although I had never ventured inside any of them. I had gone plenty of times with Morgan and my father to the edge of the largest cave, nicknamed Sunny Jim. You could descend the 145 steps from the cliff down into the cave. The seven caves all had interesting names with their own unique histories. Pirates used some of them; one, named Sea Surprise, was filled with the fossilized remains of creatures. I guessed that I was in the Arch Cave, the second largest cave that sits just left of Sunny Jim and its 145 steps to the surface. I needed to get to those steps, but I'd have to swim out of this cave and back into what was now high tide to reach the entrance. With the current, it wasn't even safe for kayakers. I would most likely be swept into jagged rocks and drown. I had one other option to the surface: the last cave, called White Lady, which had a beach with ropes leading back up to the coastal trail. If I could reach that, I could climb up the slope otherwise known as The Devil's Slide.

The White Lady cave was named after a tragedy that occurred during the 1800s: a large wave swept away a beautiful newlywed collecting seashells and carried her into the cave. Some say she was still wearing her wedding dress, and that the opening of the cave looked like her figure. I always wondered why there was so much detail about how beautiful she was and her stunning blue eyes—like it was more of a tragedy that she died because she was pretty. There were lots of rescues in the caves. I was determined to be one of them. I wouldn't meet the White Lady's fate if I could help it.

The tide continued to rise in my cave, and the sea lion barked at me as more sea lions swam into the cave. Even though I was not a fan of being on the beach, I had never had a problem with pools. I was a good swimmer. The cool, crisp water calmed my senses. Water had been a constant, underappreciated friend. I eased into the water, swimming slowly, trying to manage the current.

Mama sea lions and their pups swam into the cave as I swam out. As they brushed past me, I realized their slick skin was rougher than I thought. Once out in the water, I would have to swim to my right and avoid the side of the cliffs. The distance between the cave openings was not far. It was navigating the hidden rocks along the edge, the variety of marine life traveling the coves, and the treacherous waves that frightened me. I could feel Morgan talking to me. He knew I was in the cove. I could do it. My Emerson rang in my ears: "Plunge into the sublime seas. Dive deep and swim far so you shall come back with self-respect, with new power. With an advanced experience that shall explain and overlook the old."

I was doing it! I was making my way around the 75-million-year-old sandstone cliff. Close to the edges of the cliffs, the algae seemed to cling to everything. I tried not to focus on the overwhelming slimy sensation that would have normally stopped me from moving forward. I was cold again, and my stamina wasn't holding. As I neared this cave, there was a shift in the color of water. It seemed darker and gray, with not a single garibaldi. I reached the entrance to the nearest cave, Sea Surprise. I clung to the side of the sandstone, trying to catch my breath. I needed a break. In front of me the water had little ripples, and I saw a back-and-forth pattern. My eyes focused on what the grayness was. Sharks. Lots of little sharks.

In my heart I had known there could be sharks. I was privy to every story that had ever reached the news about shark attacks in this area. Sea lions, kayakers, access to the open water, and the rising temperature of the ocean in Mexico made it a great place for all the marine life to converge. I once saw video of a hammerhead shark nudging a kayaker near the opening to these caves. I knew sharks had to survive, and they were just doing their thing, but my empathy was with the baby seals born safe within the caves, unaware of what might wait for them if they dipped in the water. I felt very much like a baby seal, unprotected. My heart was racing, but it wasn't fueling my movement. I was stuck on this bit of craggy rock. The waves were unforgiving, and my body smacked into the side of a sharp-edged piece of shell or rock that I couldn't see. The surrounding water became tinged with my blood. I felt like I was on the couch screaming at a character in a horror movie: "Get out of the water. Get in the cave. That's blood. Sharks. Blood. We've all seen that episode." This time the girl on the screen—me—heard. I moved quickly into Sea Surprise and climbed up onto the side and out of the water. I examined my cut. It was tiny, but it produced lots of blood. I applied pressure. The pain made me more alert.

I was grateful that it wasn't dark yet. Now that the moon had finished its business with the sun that caused the eclipse, the sun shone extra bright, as if to pronounce its return to supremacy or to reassure us lowly earth inhabitants that everything could return to normal. Nothing would ever be normal again for me, but I was grateful for the rays of light that forced their way through every crack and crevice of this sea cave. As the light shone down on me, I prayed. A small quiet prayer. In church they talked about faith, and in magazine articles science tried to quantify what faith and prayer do to the brain and body. Even if it was placebo effect, lots of research dollars and MRIs have tracked that something happens in the minds and bodies of believers—no matter what faith they practice. I was instantly calm. People take it for granted that we can transport images from faraway signals to our TVs, phones, and computer screens. Do we really know how any of that happens or why it can happen or why we need it to happen? My message and my prayer I sent up to the heavens was simple: "Please."

I looked around the cave. It was rumored to have about 80 feet of walking passage beyond the entrance. I needed to move, to stay warm. I walked further into the cave. I didn't see any sea life at all. The water was clear and shallow, with dense round rocks on the floor of the cave. The sides and top of the cave were orange tinged, and erosion had created smooth layers with hints of fossilized creatures embedded deep within the sandstone. I was getting colder and sneezed. I heard the echo of my sneeze reverberate through the cave. I hadn't even thought about calling out for help in here. Maybe a kayaker, snorkeler, or hiker on the surface could hear me!

"Morgan! Morgan!" I shouted with both my actual voice and my mind. My voice echoed back to me from a seemingly far off location. I continued to call. My voice was getting hoarse, but I would call until nightfall and beyond if I had to. I had given up hope of swimming to the White Lady until it was low tide. Low tide would come a few hours before moonrise, which would be after midnight. So I would have time between the beginning of low tide and sunrise for optimal water levels, but I wasn't about to enter the water in the dark. I would head out at sunrise, or I would have to try one last push before sunset. I paced in the cave, trying to stay warm. I looked at the walls. I prayed. I screamed. I shouted. Every once in a while I heard a ripple in the water and would look and see nothing. So I continued my cycle.

I was just about to scream once more when I heard a giggle. I turned around quickly and saw them. I was being watched. A large fish that looked like a cross between a koi and the garibaldi was swimming back and forth, watching me. I stopped and sat by the water's edge to watch it watch me. It surfaced and paused in one spot, watching me, then it giggled with bubbles that floated up into the cave.

"Hello, little fish." Something told me to touch the fish. I reached out and pet it like it was a dog or cat. The fish glowed and transformed into a little Asian boy who climbed out of the water dressed in a simple tan tunic.

"Hello." It was startling, but after my day, I was happy not to be alone. The little boy hugged me. He was apparently happy to not be alone either.

"I'm so glad you can see me! I have been stranded here for ever so long!"

I frowned. "I'm feeling like that might be my fate. I'm trying to make it back to the surface and out of these caves. Why don't you just swim out?"

"The sharks. They're waiting for me. Generations of sharks have been waiting for me. They have a score to settle." Sharks with an agenda would go against everything shark-loving environmentalists would have us believe. The idea that sharks could hold a grudge and come back for years and pass that hate on to their children seemed improbable if not impossible. I introduced myself before digging deeper into what this boy had to say.

"I'm Muriel."

He bowed and responded. "I am Bo." I stood up and bowed back. I felt stiff and cold, so I stretched a bit and jumped in place.

"What are you doing?"

"I'm trying to keep my blood flowing. I'm super cold."

"May I?" He extended a hand to me. I nodded that he could touch me. He sent a blast of warmth through my body. Just what I needed to be clear and hear it. Morgan was at the top of the cliff. He was waiting for me, trying to figure out how to get me. He was going to try the descent down into Sunny Jim cave, but they had blocked the entrance because of high tide.

"So why can't we swim out of here again? I think with your help we could make it."

"The sharks."

"Well, I'll need to try before the tide gets any higher. Other than sharks' regular motives of trying to get food, why do they have a problem with you?"

Bo faced the cave wall and painted a picture on it as he talked. He drew a picture of people in Chinese dress stepping onto an ancient vessel and being herded like cattle into tight spaces. Then he drew the ocean and the rough sea voyage. The boat dropped anchor, and the passengers swam with their belongings strapped to their backs into the sea cave. As the passengers made their way into the cave, sharks guarding the entrance of the cave attacked them. Bo showed himself transforming into a fish and luring the sharks away from the entrance. The people made it into the cave, and the boat sailed away. Bo transformed back into a boy and joined them in the cave. His last drawing showed hundreds of baby sharks and the travelers spearing them and eating them. I knew that La Jolla's shores were renowned for the harmless, pregnant, tiny-mouthed leopard sharks that arrived in June to give birth in the calm shallow waters. I had never heard stories about the bigger sharks doing the same thing, but I knew they visited the shores whenever they wanted.

"This was their nursery. It was a sacred place for all shark races. The immigrants were left here hiding, and smugglers started using it as a regular spot until it was no longer sacred or safe for the shark people. Since I am a water being, they felt it to be a betrayal in favor of humankind."

"So you have been hiding here ever since?"

"He's not hiding. He's in captivity." I instantly recognized the voice of Calliope. My heart leaped with joy! Bo quickly jumped into the water and turned back into a fish.

"Where is Morgan? And what do you mean, captivity?"

Bo spit water at Calliope, getting her feathers wet. "I didn't know. I have paid my debt. I should be free."

"Morgan is here."

I turned my attention back to Bo. "So why were you here with them? Why were you on the boat?"

"Many of us travelled with our people during the gold rush. I have relatives who are human, just like you do."

"I am human."

Bo giggled like he did when he first saw me. "Part-human. Like me. Like her."

Calliope quickly corrected him.

"I am not human. I only appear like it."

I tried to process this information. I guessed if my mother was a mermaid, then I was part mermaid? I hadn't traveled down this thought stream yet. I hadn't had a moment to think about what this meant for me and Morgan. Were we mermaids too? Would we eventually meet my mother's same fate and become wild creatures of the sea? No, that must be avoided at all costs. I needed to stay focused. I was getting out of here, and Bo would help me. I didn't care what Calliope's opinions were about what had happened a hundred years ago. I was getting out of here, and fish boy would help me.

"Bo, we're both going to get out of here. You were only trying to help your family. I know it's complex, but nobody deserves to be isolated in captivity forever." Calliope shook her head in disappointment.

"This will not earn you favor with your people. The people who will help you find your mother."

"My people are Morgan and everyone waiting for me on the surface. No one is going to stop me from finding my mother and bringing her home." Bo excitedly leaped from the water and shifted back into boy form.

"Calliope, what is keeping him here?"

"Nothing. He was enchanted at first, but after that he could have swum out long ago if he wanted to risk being eaten. It's his cowardice and guilt that have kept him prisoner."

Bo nodded his head. "I didn't want to be torn to shreds."

"Have you tried talking to them? Have you apologized?"

"No, I never have," Bo responded.

Calliope stared at us with an air of superiority.

"These sharks will not forgive him. The legend has grown too long. He has missed his chance. I promise you he has no chance." I pulled Bo to the side and talked softly in his ear.

"Are you truly sorry?"

"Yes. I didn't know what this place was and am sorry for their sacrifice." I looked deep into his eyes and could feel the sincerity. He had suffered long enough, and I needed to get to my brother.

"Where will you go when you leave this place? The land or sea?"

"I'll journey up the coast and eventually back to my home sea."

"Calliope, can you please talk to the sharks and let them know that he wants to talk—but to only one of them. The rest need to keep their distance." I whispered my plan in Bo's ear as Calliope stood at the edge of the cave talking to the sharks. She quickly returned.

"They have agreed to listen, but not to forgive. This may be the moment they exact their revenge." Bo stayed in human form, and we walked to the water's edge. I picked up a small rock. We both slid gently into the water, keeping our eye on the lone shark. The shark got close.

Bo shouted and cried frantically. "I'm ever so sorry! I didn't know this place was sacred. Please let me go."

The shark showed his layered shark-tooth grin and moved in for the kill. I was in his sights. As the shark closed in, I motioned for Bo to change forms. The shark lunged at us. I rammed my rock into its nose and caught a ride with Bo out of our cave entrance, and we sprinted to the White Lady Cave. Sharks closed in and tried to corner us.

"Bo, swim faster!"

The high tide swirled around us, and the sharks were within striking range. I wouldn't be able to get in another cheap shot. Our swimming kicked into high gear, and we neared the cave known as Little Sister, which was shaped like the opening to the White Lady Cave but smaller. One more cave to go. I looked ahead and then down to see sharks coming up near my feet. Then I could no longer see anything around me but orange.

I noticed the flowing pectoral fins of the plump little red-orange fish. Hundreds of them, some bright orange, others with small spots of blue, coming to our rescue. We were within a ball of fish. They swam up and around us as we moved forward, keeping pace and disguising us. The ones on the edge of the ball charged at the approaching sharks and made a grunting noise that sounded much like a little burp. They focused their yellow eyes on the intruders, our predators. The garibaldi of the area had united, protecting their territory. They must have had a grudge of their own to settle with the sharks.

Our allies filled the water with their orange frenzy. We kept moving forward. The outpouring of aggressive fish support stunned the sharks. White sea spray crashed against the rocks as we reached the White Lady Cave. I could see the resemblance to a woman in a billowy white dress made of sea mist. As quickly as they had appeared, the garibaldi vanished. We were safely out of the reach of the sharks. Bo called out into the water.

"Thank you! I really am sorry!"

We were now at the easternmost corner of the sea cliff. White Lady had a small beach-type area with big rocks and some sand. There were static ropes hanging over the slippery slope, the "Devil's Slide." At the top of the slope was a small wooden bridge that connected to the coastal trail. Bo and I stood at the bottom, looking up. We knew we couldn't make it up the side of the sandstone cliff. We'd made it as far as we could go. The tide was high, and tall waves crashed against the large rocks. Even the interior of the cave was becoming inaccessible. I noticed a light above. I waved and shouted. Morgan was there! I could hear him again in my heart.

"We're here, Muri." There were rescue crews with Morgan at the top of the cliff. I turned to Bo.

"What are we going to say about you?"

Bo gave me a hug. "I'm diving in and swimming north. The sharks have turned back, and I'm free to find my way again. Thank you, Muriel. Maybe I'll see you again!"

"Bo—If you meet a mermaid named Lorelei along the way, let her know that we will find her and bring her home. Nothing will stop that."

The flashlight beams danced on the water and rocks as the crew rappelled down the slippery rock. Bo dove in and transformed into his fish self and swam quickly away before they saw him. The team of rescuers secured me and lifted me up the side of the Devil's Slide. I was up on top of the cliff and out of harm's way within seconds. Morgan, Spencer, and my dad were at the top of the cliff. My dad rushed to me. The rescuers motioned for him to move back so they could remove the safety harness and other gear from my body. Once I was free of it, I ran to him. His embrace was warm and reassuring. Everything would be all right. He brushed the hair out of my face and looked sternly at me.

"What were you doing kayaking alone? You don't even kayak." I looked over at Morgan, wondering what cover story he had given my father, and why? Hadn't he told him about Mom? Morgan joined us.

"Dad, I told you. We were planning on meeting her. There was just a mix-up. We were going to check out the eclipse together from the shores." I nodded.

"I guess I thought they would show up."

"But you don't even like the water!"

"I don't mind the water. It's the beach that bugs me."

He held me tight. "Okay, okay. let's just go home. You know you missed my show."

"Yes, I'm sorry. How did it go?"

"It went really well. I just wish your mother could have been here to see it."

The rescue crew checked me out and cleared me to go home. I got a stern talking-to from the team, and they reminded me how much money these types of rescues cost the taxpayers of California. I apologized profusely and swore I would never do anything so reckless again—although I knew that it was only the beginning of what I might have to endure to find my mother. I think we were going to have to redefine things in terms of necessary risk. Morgan pushed a thought into my mind.

"Dad somehow believes that Mom has been missing for a while."

I said nothing.

Back at the house, my dad tucked me in beneath several blankets on the sofa. He directed Morgan and Spencer to look after me while he wrapped up the details of the opening of his show. He kissed a picture of my mother on the way out the door.

"I wish you could have been here, Lorelei."

Morgan pressed his finger to his lips. He could tell I was about to confront my father about what was really going on with my mother. Morgan peeked through the curtains, making sure that my father was gone. Spencer sat down next to me on the sofa.

"We went straight from Paradise Point to your dad. We told him everything. He thought Morgan was hysterical."

Morgan sat down on the other side of me. "He thinks Mom has been missing since Aunt Mallory's incident. The whole thing has been rewritten in his mind."

There was a knock at the door, but they didn't wait for us to answer. We heard them let themselves in. It was Brooke. Morgan leaped up to confront her.

"What are you doing here? I know you remember what just went down."

Brooke had an overstuffed messenger bag with her and a few books in her arms. She looked confused by this comment.

"How are you going to help?" I shouted at her.

"Well, I brought you some books and stuff I think you left at my place since I don't recognize them. They look like they're from the library."

Spencer looked Brooke up and down. "I don't trust her. Her cool Hawaiian vibe seems to be totally gone."

Brooke scrunched her face up and dropped the books and messenger bag on the table. "You're right, Spencer—I have changed. I don't enjoy hanging out with you *haoles*. Maybe my dad's right—we should go back to Hawaii. You guys have been so weird."

The three of us stared at Brooke. I lashed out. "How are we weird? After what you've done. You should go back to Hawaii!"

"Muri—I get it. I really do. I miss my mom too, but you guys are *maha'oi*." Brooke flashed the shaka sign sarcastically and left, slamming the door behind her. "*Mahalo.*"

I hadn't told Morgan and Spencer about my encounter with my mother in the ocean. Now I wasn't sure where to start since things were like an episode of *The Twilight Zone*. Brooke didn't have any idea about what was happening, or at least that's how it seemed.

I picked up the bag and books and sat down on the floor, spreading out all the resource material. There were copies of newspaper articles, books, maps, and a few pictures. Morgan and Spencer sat down next to me and started sorting through items. There were details about the curse and strange information about how to kill a mermaid. Iron was dangerous to their health in large concentrations, and iron weapons could keep them away from ships and land. But "sky-iron" (meteoric iron) was deadly. An injury from a weapon forged of iron infused with the celestial properties always proved fatal to not only mermaids, but all nephilim. I do think my mother was ill in part because of all the metal in our home. Then I discovered an article about a 1967 Canadian ferry ride. The article described a sighting of a mermaid on Mayne Island, British Columbia, as passengers went by on a ferry traveling the Active Pass shipping channel. The event happened at dusk and was seen by passengers on several ferries. Eyewitnesses described the mermaid as having long silver-blonde hair. Some said she was holding a large fish. A few people took pictures. I handed the article to Morgan.

"Colin must have believed this was our mother and grandmother." Morgan and Spencer looked closely at the article and the accompanying photo. I opened a book on Bible interpretations of the word nephilim.

There was another news clipping, an account of a fisherman finding a baby wrapped in sea grass near the San Juan Islands off the coast of Washington state. The fisherman was from a town called Friday Harbor.

Morgan read it and shook his head at this information. "Mom said she was from the Pennsylvania area."

Spencer looked at the picture. "If people saw a mermaid in 1967 and took pictures, why have we never heard of it? No one believes in mermaids," Spencer asked.

I held open a book on water deities that was in the nephilim tome. "It looks like people have believed in mermaids for a very long time. Every culture on the planet has a story about some sort of merperson."

Spencer was skeptical. "We would know."

Morgan threw his hands in the air and paced. "Okay. Okay. We know that mermaids exist. Our mother turned into one before our eyes a few hours ago. What are we doing talking about proof of mermaids? We have to find her!"

"That's what I'm trying to figure out. If she's headed home, wouldn't this be home? Not where she told us she grew up, but where she was born?"

"And how are we going to get there? We'd need access to the open ocean. She won't be hanging out on the island."

Spencer smiled. "We have a boat, and I can sail her."

"You mean your parents have a boat."

"That's just a technicality."

Morgan looked intrigued. "How would we take it out?"

"My parents are leaving tomorrow for a conference. Don't tell the world, but they were letting me stay on my own. My grandpa is keeping tabs on me, but he's not staying with me." Morgan pulled up a coastal map on his phone. He tracked tides and the surf to optimize the best times to be in the water.

"Even if we could get the boat, it's a long haul and rough water. If we're going, I think we're flying to Washington."

"What about Calliope? Do you think she'll help?" I was desperate for any advantage.

"She doesn't really tell us much of anything. It's like she's teasing us with information," Morgan declared, frustrated.

"Calliope doesn't work for us. She and her siren sisters have to answer to every nephilim that calls them. They are bound by an oath to help as far as they can without interfering." I pointed to information in the book. There was a drawing that looked very much like a siren. "That means they don't know everything, because others don't want them to share their desires."

"What did Colin have to gain in getting Mom?"

"I'm not sure. But I wish we could ask Brooke." I shuffled the papers and analyzed everything, hoping something would give me an answer.

"Yes! How did saving the coral reef turn into your aunt's a mermaid?" Spencer snidely remarked. Spencer jingled his keys. "Are we catching a plane?"

Morgan looked at a picture of my parents on the table in the hallway. We were trying to figure out just who Colin was...and what was his role other than finding mermaids and returning them to the water?

"Is it just us going, or are we trying to get Dad on board?" Morgan pondered how productive it would be.

"So does everyone else remember Mom? Can we just show him the hospital discharge papers?"

"It's like she really has been gone for a year. There is nothing. Her closet is empty. They have erased her up to the point we lost Aunt Mallory."

With the mention of Aunt Mallory, my heart filled with sorrow for everyone's loss. My poor cousin who I really loved deeply—I knew her grief all year. Her mother really was never coming back. I could feel her pain. We still had a chance of seeing our mother again. As I took a deep breath, it was like water was filling my lungs. Our connection hadn't been broken—I was not only empathetic to Morgan, but I could feel Brooke. I guess I felt Bo as well. Was I an empath now? Had I always been one? Is that why I was always so overwhelmed? This was exactly what I would not want to be. I already felt too much. Now I felt like Brooke was in trouble and that we needed to find her.

Morgan answered my thought. "I'm not going after her. My priority is Mom."

"Spence, can I have a ride? I think Brooke is in trouble."

Spencer shrugged and looked at Morgan.

"You cool with it?"

"Whatever you think you need to do. I'm planning a trip." Morgan had his phone out and several maps showing Mayne Island and the San Juan Islands.

Spencer and I raced to the car. I felt weak and tired. The ordeal of the day was settling into my body. Every moment that passed, I felt more overwhelmed to the point of inaction, but I got into the car.

"Where to?" Spencer could tell I wasn't feeling well. "Maybe you should stay here? Just tell me where you think I need to go."

"No, I'm coming. Let's go to her surf spot. That's where she is."

Spencer drove the short distance to Brooke Kainoa's favorite spot to surf and commune with the sea. Brooke found the spot, located near the rocks where I had seen her kissing Colin, when she first came to San Diego to live. She would climb on her board and just float at first. She wasn't ready to re-engage with the waves. She once told me she wasn't sure how she felt about the ocean anymore. Then one day she swam out and took a wave. She remembered what it was like to move in unison with the sea—to be swept along and made part of its ebb and flow. She was connected to her mother when she was in the water.

We stood on the edge of the water looking into the dark. The sun had set long ago. The moon and the streetlights provided just enough light to see Brooke's board. I pointed to the board. Spencer could see it.

"I don't see Brooke—do you see Brooke?" I shouted over the loud crashing waves. Spencer pointed to a body floating out in the water. It looked like her hand was resting on the board, but she wasn't swimming.

"We've got to go in after her." I tried to muster up the energy to dive into the water, but I had no strength. I felt like I was sinking into the water as I merely sat on the water's edge. Spencer dove in quickly and fought the waves to reach Brooke. I soon saw the problem: Brooke was in a riptide and Spencer had just dove into it. The current was carrying Brooke farther from the shore, and Spencer was struggling, trying to find the way to out-swim the current to reach her. Our parents and PSAs taught us to swim parallel to the rip current as it attempted to take you out to deep water. Spencer realized he was swimming in a current, taking him seaward. He swam parallel to the beach, trying to escape the deadly flow. The water was traveling in a huge circle. Brooke seemed to go with the flow, and she and her board were making their way back in closer but on the opposite side of the rip from where Spencer was struggling. I could see him struggling, beginning to panic as the exhaustion claimed him. Stuck on the sidelines, watching, I called out for help. I called out to Morgan. I called out to the street. I called out to the ocean. I prayed and prayed.

"Dear Lord, help us!" Morgan was already on his way riding my bike, Butter. He had sensed my distress and came after me. He had come for me, not Brooke. He climbed quickly to where I was and was about to jump in, but I grabbed his arm.

"They're in a riptide. You can't get in here. You'll jump right into it."

Morgan looked around for another entry point, but before he could get in, help arrived. The water shimmered in the moonlight. The surface looked like an oil slick, and the spray was a brief rainbow. Two shimmery purple, blue, yellow, orange, and green tails splashed in the water. They looked less like scales and more like watercolor waves of rainbow light. I recognized them as my new reality: mermaids.

They swam to the victims of the powerful current. A raven-haired young beauty with golden seashells, pearls, and starfish braided in her flowing hair scooped up Spencer and swam him back to shore. Spencer, adrenaline-high from panic, at first resisted until she hummed a soothing tune and he relaxed into her arms and recognized her beauty. Spellbound by her essence, he clung tightly to her neck. Her top half was dressed in gauze-like sea sponge and shells.

The second mermaid looked very much like the first one but slightly older, and her hair was almost the same color as her tail. She was like a gliding rainbow through the waves. She placed an unconscious Brooke on her surfboard and glided her to where we were waiting. Her hair was dressed with simple tiny white starfish and what looked like live seahorses moving about in her locks of hair. I helped pull Brooke out of the water. My energy was returning. I held her close to me and hugged her. She spit up water and opened her eyes. She saw her rescuer and moved quickly away from the water. I held her, reassuring her.

"You're okay. She saved you." I got up and moved to the water's edge.

"Thank you."

"You're welcome. We heard your call. I am Luna, and this is my younger sister Stella." Stella handed Spencer to Morgan and then addressed me. She had a hostile, agitated tone. My impression of her shifted as she lost the demeanor that went along with her calming, musical rescue of Spencer.

I introduced our group: "Hello, I'm Muriel, this is Brooke, Spencer, and Morgan."

"Why didn't you dive in and save them?" she asked with disdain. I looked at Morgan, and Spencer, stunned.

"If I could have, I would have. Not even Spencer was able to handle the riptide."

Luna stepped in to apologize for her sister. "She asks because we were answering the call of another sister of the sea. We thought you were injured and in need of our help. Then we saw these humans." She then addressed Stella and pointed to Morgan. "You see, they are changelings, dear sister." She pointed to Morgan. Stella had already been sizing up Morgan with approval. I wouldn't have been surprised if she reached out and stroked his hair like the rest of the mortal girls. The disturbing piece was that Spencer was looking wistfully at Stella, as if he wanted to climb back into her embrace.

"This is your brother, correct?"

"Yes, but we're not changelings—whatever they are. We simply have a mermaid mom. We just found out today, so pretty new development," Morgan chimed in.

Luna shook her head. "No, I can tell there is more than that. You have some other magic."

Brooke spoke up. Her eyes seemed cleared of the haze. She looked at me with terror and a recognition of what she had done. "Oh! Muri, oh no! What have we done?"

Morgan ignored Brooke and her hysteria and instead spoke to the mermaid.

"Well, we are all subject to a curse from an ancestor that had an encounter with a mermaid hundreds of years ago."

Stella shook her head. "No, I do not see it in these humans we saved. They have no magic. Just you."

Brooke stared off into the distance—into the sea. I sneered at Stella. "You don't know what you're talking about. What's the deal, are there mermaids freaking everywhere and we've just never seen them before today?"

Luna answered my question. "Yes. There are lots of things under the sea I'm sure you've never seen before. We are travelling to Hong Kong with our pod."

Spencer was in awe of the mermaids and what they were saying. He had a hundred questions he could barely contain.

"How do you speak our language? Why Hong Kong? How many

are in your pod? Are they all girls, I mean mermaids? Why don't your scales seem like scales? How old are you? What types of creatures live under the sea with you?"

Stella answered quickly without taking her eyes off Morgan. "We speak all languages. The pink dolphins are dying in Hong Kong, and we are trying to help them with safe passage. I don't know. Seventeen. Creatures that would be happy to eat you." Stella sighed and looked to Morgan as he asked his question.

"My mother is said to be a wild mermaid. She transformed today during the eclipse and knows nothing of the mer-people. Do you know how we can find her?"

Both Stella and Luna seemed frightened by this information. Luna pulled herself out of the water onto the rocks, revealing her luminous torso and tail. Her skin was covered with patches of algae, and the sea-horses in her hair were definitely alive and moving. She motioned for me to come closer, and she talked in a quiet whisper.

"Is your mother the mermaid, Lorelei?" She looked deep in my eyes with concern.

"Yes! She is. How do you know? Where is she?"

She motioned to Stella to return completely to the water. Stella pulled away from the rocks. She sang a soft little song as she swam away. "I hope to see you again Morgan, son of Lorelei." With that, she dove deep and swam far out of sight.

"Muriel, do not seek her out. It will not be a happy ending for you." Her eyes flashed like the dark seal eyes my mother had at La Jolla Shores. She looked around quickly and listened to the wind. She made several clicks and whistles like the ones my mother made. The wind caught her hair. In this moment I realized I'd told no one that I spent a moment face to face with the mermaid version of my mother and that she knew me. She knew me for a brief moment.

"Morgan, I saw Mom in the cove. She knew me. I don't know why I didn't tell you before. But then she changed and looked like this for a moment and was gone. Dolphins and a merman captured her. I know this sounds crazy, and I guess I was still in shock or denial about the whole thing! And processing that Dad doesn't remember exactly what happened to mom." Luna's body caught the moonlight, and the oily reflective colors were almost blinding. The spray around the rocks looked like it was all rainbows. Luna's wildness brought out a wildness in me. I wasn't afraid of her creature quality, and I grabbed her by the shoulders and shook her.

"Where is my mother? I command you to tell me!" I wasn't sure why I used those exact words, but her eyes returned to a light sea green and she was with me again. At first she was angered by me and my harsh treatment.

"You cannot command me, any more than the wind and waves command me!" I removed my hands from her shoulders, and she slipped back into the water.

"I'm sorry. Please help us! Please. We must find our mother."

Morgan came to my side. "Please help us."

Luna became very quiet again.

"Your mother is traveling far from these waters. She is returning to her origin place and being reunited with her family."

"Where is this place? Is it where she was born?"

"Yes." She then whispered softly and sang as she swam away, "We expect your mother to do great things. We've been waiting for her a very long time. Goodbye, children of Lorelei." We watched her swim off into the distance. She stayed close to the surface, and the moon reflected off her tail as if it were chasing the rainbow.

We were all wet from the spray, tired and cold. We needed to just regroup and figure it out. We needed to go home, cuddle up on the couch, and watch cooking shows just like Mom would do. We needed to get my father to see what was going on.

We drove home exhausted, and all sat shell-shocked on the couch, but I wasn't ready to concede the day. Once we were within the safety of our four walls, I called out.

"Calliope, Mel, and whoever the third one was hanging out on the boat today."

It was almost midnight and my father had yet to return. I wouldn't mind if he walked in and saw these sirens in my living room. At least it would open the conversation as to where Mom was, and that she hadn't died in the boating accident with Aunt Mallory. The three sirens appeared in our living room. We could all see them. Brooke and Spencer were woken up to the different layers of our reality, and they could see just as we could. Calliope was the first one to speak. She seemed to find everything so amusing. Which did not amuse me.

"Ha, you have called us again. I see you survived the cave. I hope for your sake you don't meet a shark anytime soon." Morgan looked at me, wondering about the threat. Calliope noticed the look.

"Oh, she hasn't told you? When she was stuck in the sea cave, she helped a changeling who was being held for crimes against sharks. She helped him escape." Calliope primped her feathers.

"He helped me escape, is the truth of it," I retorted. Morgan held my hand.

"If she helped him, then she made the right choice. I trust her judgment."

"So you need to come clean about everything you know. We're leaving in the morning to find our mother." As I spoke, Brooke stood up and held my other hand. She asked Calliope the next question.

"Why can't our fathers remember that Lorelei was here yesterday?"

"Because Colin is a powerful believer and he has them clouded. It will last for only a short time, but long enough for her to be well on her way."

"A believer? What's a believer?" Spencer chimed in. Melpomene answered this question.

"A believer is someone who has been gifted with the knowledge of our past origin story and our future potential. They believe that God created the heavens and oceans. There was a great storm that swelled the ocean and destroyed many evil beings. There was a rainbow covenant with man that the waters would never be used again in such a way, by the heavens."

Spencer was quick to respond. "Yes, Noah's ark. Everyone's heard that story before. Even if they don't believe it. It's part of popular culture. You know, animals saved two by two." The third silent siren, who I had avoided eye contact with, stepped in front of Calliope and Melpomene. There was something about her that made me nervous. When we were on the boat, I had seen her watching everything without being involved. I didn't like her eyes on me then, and I definitely didn't like it now. I regretted having included her in my call. It was the first time I had gotten a good look at her, and I noticed she had angel wings like Mel, but very different from Calliope's bird-like structure. Her wings were black and her skin was like an albino's. This was Raidne, the last siren I would ever meet.

She spoke with a deep, cool voice. Everything she said was matter of fact. She addressed her sisters first.

"I know you have accepted your fate of bouncing from nephilim to nephilim, doing their bidding, keeping their secrets, and just waiting to see what happens. You must have realized by now it's pointless!" She then looked at me and Morgan.

"Listen well—so we can be done with you. Colin and his kind believe that the destruction of the world by fire as predicted in your Bible is coming to pass and being caused by man's own hand. The oceans are heating, and fires blaze on land. Our people made it through the flood, of course, but will not make it through the fire, so he wants to tip the scales literally in our favor. There are three mermaids predicted to be able to control the water and the wind. They can cause hurricanes and typhoons and level the earth by tsunami. The result would be most or all of the earth covered by water. This would minimize the effect of man's destruction."

Spencer was instantly concerned for the human race since he was part of it. Morgan was more interested in how our mother played into this whole scenario.

"So he wants to kill off mankind?"

Raidne responded with an irritated tone. "No, just decrease the population to manageable levels. I have foretold many plagues that have done this very thing."

"And what about our mother, Lorelei?"

"She's one of the mermaids. Her mother is another one. We don't know who the third one is." She turned to her sisters.

"Okay, ladies, let's go." Then she looked deep into my eyes.

"Don't call me again."

With that, she fluffed her black wings and was about to leave when Morgan continued, "How do you know it's our mom that's this mermaid?"

"She is—but no one knows how she was so cleverly hidden and kept within the Lutey spell, hiding her true identity." She then turned to Brooke. "I guess we owe you a debt of gratitude."

And with that quip, she vanished. Calliope and Mel came closer to Morgan and me. I could feel some warmth or love coming from them toward us. They didn't seem to feel the same way as Raidne. Each of the sirens opened her hands. Calliope had a small comb, much like the one my mother was wearing in her hair and that we had used to call Calliope. She handed it to Morgan.

"You may call for help from a mermaid or other sea creature by running this comb through the sand and sea."

Mel's hand had a small mirror made of red coral and seashells. She handed it to me.

"This will show you some things, but be careful—it is just a glimpse, never the whole story. Act wisely based on what you see."

The front door opened. For one moment, my father saw the two remaining sirens. He stared, processing what was happening in his living room. Calliope smiled at him and kissed Morgan on the cheek; then with a blink she was no longer there. I was starting to think Calliope had a favorite. Morgan and his charms were working their way into an even wider realm. You had to give it to him, since I knew he wasn't even trying to charm every female human or nephilim within a five-mile radius. Mel left the moment she knew my father had spied her. My father was shaky and looked like he might come crashing down. Spencer ran over to support him, and Brooke grabbed a chair. He stared off into the distance and began to cry.

"Your mother is alive, isn't she? I remember. I just brought her home from the hospital yesterday." He leaped out of the chair. "She's alive! Where is she? What were those creatures?"

Morgan helped my dad back into the chair. "Dad, I tried to tell you earlier. We really don't have time for a whole explanation now. I'm glad you remember Mom. Now we have to go save her. We can explain on the way."

"On the way where?" He was still so bewildered by his conflicting memories, the story Morgan had told him earlier in the day, and witnessing the sirens standing in our living room.

"Get your frequent flyer miles out. We're going to Washington State to find Mom."

Brooke looked sheepishly at the group. "I'd like to come, but I think I've caused enough trouble." My dad looked at her with disdain. "Did you and your father really dump my wife in the ocean?" She hung her head and nodded with shame. I put my arms around her.

"Dad, she knows it was wrong, but I get it now. She was just desperate for Aunt Mallory. Your sister. You know what it feels like."

Morgan held a hard line. "Just go home to your father. None of us are ready to forgive you yet."

My father softened. "We'll work it out when we get back. We're still family."

Morgan stormed out of the room. "Nice way to back me up, Dad—classic."

Spencer had been sending messages on his phone. "I've already got me covered. My grandpa is off the hook from watching me, and my parents are good if I'm with you, Mr. Lutey."

Brooke smiled meekly, and this time she meant her "*mahalo*" as she left.

We were all in agreement. We wasted no more time. My dad checked flights. I grabbed the books and shoved them into a duffel with everything I thought I might need. I realized that I was overpacking and freaking out. Morgan noticed it when I packed a third bottle of sunblock, snorkel, and hand sanitizer.

"I'm sure if we have to dive, there will be equipment there. We can also rent a boat there." His logic soothed me.

"Yes, and Dad's with us now." Then I freaked out again. "But what can he really do?"

"If we see Mom, maybe he can get through to her. I know you think I don't know everything that happened out there in the cove, but I was with you. I could hear bits and pieces of it. That's why we were waiting for you at the top. I know you tried to get through to her." He gave me an old-time bigger-brother bear hug. I missed this guy. I didn't know why we had been fighting our connection for so long. He was in my head, and I knew his heart. We could do this together. My dad rushed into the room.

"We've got to catch the last flight out tonight. There's a tropical cyclone forming into a Pacific hurricane. I guess the northern Pacific hasn't seen a storm like this since Patsy in 1959."

"How are we going to find Mom in a hurricane?" I paced and threw an extra bottle of sunscreen in my bag.

"Maybe we should consider asking Uncle Nohea to help us? He could give us updates on the weather. He does work for the National Oceanic Atmospheric Administration."

"No, let's go." Morgan and I looked at each other and were amazed by our father's quick action on the airplane tickets. Everything we had thought about our parents' relationship was being questioned. He was devoted to her. Was she as devoted to him, or was it the Lutey power that he had held over her all of these years? His metalworking had compromised her health and not allowed her to discover her true identity. We wondered whether he could get through to her. Was his love the key to bringing her home? The metalworking—it made me think of the strange lore about harming a mermaid.

"Dad, I need something from your shop first." I rummaged through my dad's things and grabbed one of his first pieces crafted from iron—a beautiful ornate necklace, which had lots of movement and sharp angles to it. No one would want to wear it for fear of getting cut. I wrapped it carefully with the mirror and hid it in my snorkeling gear packed in my suitcase. I was ready. The four of us made it quickly to the airport and through the check-in process. They forced me to remove all the sunscreen from my carry-on. The agents scanning our bags were intrigued by what we were taking with us on the plane. A nosey agent looked at my ticket destination and remarked on my snorkel.

"You know there's a big storm coming. You're probably not going to get to use that," she commented.

I smiled, trying not to look annoyed. "I know, I heard." I was nervous about the metal in my bag. The agent saw it on the screen as it traveled through the X-ray machine. She unwrapped it and looked at me. She didn't bother with the mirror.

"It's very unusual." She wrapped it back up. My dad was watching.

"Yes, my dad made it. He's an artist."

The agent looked to my dad for confirmation. He nodded. "Yes, some of my early work." The agent waved us through and sent our belongings down the conveyor belt.

"It's nice. Enjoy your flight."

Once we made it out of earshot, the Lutey men questioned me. "Why do you have that, Muri?" my dad asked.

Morgan pressed questions into my mind. *"What are you thinking? Why didn't I know you packed that?"* I wondered that question myself. Maybe our connection came and went with no real reason? Or was I starting to control it? I answered them both aloud, "I thought we might need it."

We were checked in and waiting. Flights were dropping off the schedule as we watched the digital board. We crossed our fingers that the airline didn't cancel this red-eye flight. There were few people in the airport. Night crews swept and emptied garbage cans. We saw the overhead display of tomorrow's flights with cancellation after cancellation listed on the board. We hoped that my mother was where the fisherman had found her, or where the mermaid sighting was in British Columbia. If not—I didn't have a plan beyond that. I felt like she was there, but it may have just been wishful thinking. I wasn't connected to her anymore.

We boarded the half-empty plane and waited. It wasn't long before the wheels were up, and we were on our way. Two hours and forty-five minutes later we landed in Seattle at the Seattle-Tacoma International Airport. Morgan and Dad were on their phones, securing the next leg of our trip. A shuttle ride to South Lake Washington and a seaplane to Friday Harbor were on the agenda. Spencer and I schlepped our bags through the airport, so they could focus on making travel plans. It was still dark outside, and the wind was making itself known. The sun tried to make its way through the dense clouds as sunrise approached. The bad news made it to us pretty quickly. We needed to wait for the shuttle and would have to see whether the seaplanes were flying today. I was nervous. I already wasn't a fan of flying, but getting on a plane where they weigh you and your luggage to make sure the airplane can handle its passengers is extreme.

The Lutey clan, plus one, sat in the airport café with too many coffee choices for one location. Coffee for teenagers, even though common for most, was forbidden in our house. As my chin slumped into my hand, my father surprised us with cups of the world-renowned Seattle coffee.

"I guess if you're going to start drinking coffee, now is as good a time as any." He smiled and handed over packages of raw sugar and creamer. We decided not to let him know that we were not only seasoned coffee drinkers, we were grateful for the brew. We would have been going through caffeine withdrawal, and we needed to be alert for what was to come. We had no plan in place. We didn't have the name of the fisherman or any record of what my mother's name would have been before her Pennsylvania adoption. Once my dad had clarity about our situation and finally gave in to the possibility that my mother was truly a creature from the deep undersea world of mermaids, he pieced together bits of the life Lorelei had shared with him. She had told him so many stories over the years that had ended with a hazy "I don't know" to his follow-up questions he assumed that things were just too difficult for her to discuss. Now he realized that she truly didn't know how she had ended up in Pennsylvania.

What was even more interesting was that my father and she were set up on a date. We never knew that. We had always assumed they had seen each other across the room and fallen madly in love with each other in college. We knew that my mother was in the music department and was a gifted student and that my father was in the art department. We had heard about their first date and the cozy little campus pizzeria where the toppings of a whole piece of pizza had ended up on my father's lap when he took the initial cheesy bite. We knew that my father went to hear my mother play one of the pieces she composed and fell instantly under her spell. Apparently, my father had a friend in college who decided he must meet this young, talented woman named Lorelei. He was dating another woman a few years older who was acting as a patron to him, so he was hesitant. He was accustomed to the attention of the ladies, just like Morgan.

He couldn't remember any details about this friend who insisted he meet our mother. He only remembered that they had several classes together but couldn't remember his name. Also, after he and Lorelei started dating, they were inseparable, and they both lost contact with any friends who had been their companions prior to meeting. Lorelei had no family, and at the time only my grandfather was living and my dad hadn't spoken to him in years. So other than Aunt Mallory, no one was in contact with the two of them during their courtship. No outside influences other than the initial setup could be identified. I had my notepad out again and was taking copious notes. I would figure out this mystery and all of its players sooner or later. I was hoping sooner.

My father knew about his family's so-called powers over mermaids and other supernatural beings. That was part of the falling-out he had with his father. His mother had been a devout Lutheran and didn't allow such talk in the house, whereas his father dabbled in the inappropriate story or two that bordered on the mildly insane. Now my father was re-evaluating all the stories he had been told by his father growing up. Were they true? And could they help us in this situation? I listened as he told story after crazy story about our ancestors, and just jotted things down.

Our shuttle arrived, and we started our journey toward San Juan Island and the town of Friday Harbor. The sun shone brightly, and the wind was absent. It was a beautiful day to search the sea. We were still concerned that the seaplanes might not be traveling because of the weather threat. Yet when we arrived in South Lake, we noticed there were no signs of a town concerned with a coming storm. No one was boarding anything up, there was no line at the grocery store or gas station. It was business as usual. They scheduled the planes to leave several times throughout the day, arriving in different spots on the San Juan Islands. We were booked and ready to go.

The yellow seaplane that awaited us was even smaller than I had imagined. They checked our height and weight before they sorted us into spots in the plane. My father ended up in the copilot's seat. It was just us and the pilot. The take-off was shaky, and my stomach did a flip-flop. I wanted to sink to the floor of the plane. Morgan looked out the window. The pilot was a kind older native man. As we passed over the water, he explained to my father that he was part of the Samish Nation. They were part of the First Nations, or First Ones. Their people had refused to accept a reservation from the US government because they wanted to remain on their lands in the San Juan Islands. Their land was eventually taken, and their culture started to slip away. He pointed down to the water.

"Keep your eyes open for the orcas. J pod orcas are our brothers and sisters." He angled the seaplane so we could get a better look at the clear water and the life within it. As if on cue, we could see them—orcas.

"We have lost one of their mothers. They need their mothers; they keep the family together. She's not travelling with the pod anymore, which is generally a sign of death." He got choked up when he said this and stopped talking altogether, trying to regain his composure. My father stayed silent.

Morgan responded, "They are beautiful. I hope that she isn't dead. What about the fathers?"

The Samish pilot answered with pride. "They stay with the pod of their mother and help raise all the young, their nephews and nieces."

Morgan then pushed a thought into my mind. *"Look into your mirror. What do you see?"* Even though my stomach was still queasy, I pulled closer to the side and looked out the window, then looked into the small mirror. Spencer sat close enough to be a distraction, but I tried to focus.

I saw mermaids. A city under the ocean. The foundation of the massive city was a long chain of seamounts—a series of submerged extinct volcanos connected by walls of natural coral, ragged rocks, shells, metal, and wooden bits from sunken ships. Within the borders of the city, some of the volcanic islands reached the surface with places for mermaids to sun themselves and look out into the great abyss. All kinds of wild sea life traveled to and from the city. There were deep trenches that led up to the city like a protective moat. The placement of the seamounts allowed for areas of shallow clear water and hidden sea grotto pockets with room to breathe. A dolphin or mermaid or even a baby whale could take a moment unseen and catch their breath.

The city was an endless view of glittering construction, repeating seamounts along the whole of the Pacific floor. Ocean currents whisked over the edge of the seamount, carrying in fish and other resources. On the edges of the city, manta rays that looked to be eighteen or more feet across swam back and forth, snacking and guarding the entrance. I could see mermaids and mermen of all shapes and sizes and colors. Some looked more like the fish they were swimming with—their upper torsos covered with scales just like their tails. Others looked more human with intricate and ornate woven tops and braided or flowing hair adorned with jewels. Their skin tones ranged from very dark to very light, and some had coral and yellow skin, as if they wanted to camouflage with their surroundings. My vision got cloudy. Something was moving sand around and obscuring what I could see. Then I saw it: a giant Pacific octopus staring back at me. With one more swipe of its tentacles, I could see no more.

We started our descent into Friday Harbor, and I braced myself. I asked the pilot two very important questions, which he answered very simply.

"Excuse me. Is there some kind of underwater mountain system nearby? Oh, and just wondering, do your people believe in mermaids?"

The pilot laughed for a moment and then answered in a very practical manner. "I wouldn't say near, but there is something called the Emperor Seamount chain that extends from Alaska to Hawaii, or there's Cobb seamount near Gray's Harbor. It's kind of like an underwater island range. And yes, some of us believe in halfway people and others don't. I'm sure that's the same as every people who live by the sea. Please prepare for landing." He laughed one more time. I guess my question had seemed odd to him. My brother glared at me. He thought I was entering into oversharing territory.

When we landed, several messages came through on my phone. Brooke had spent her time researching and sent all the information she had gathered about mermaid sightings on the island and a picture of the old news article about the baby found at sea. It said in the article that the fisherman's relative had adopted the baby and moved to Pennsylvania. There was a brief mention about the Catholic parish of Friday Harbor, which was responsible for all the islands of the San Juan Archipelago. They had cared for the baby until it was formally adopted. This was a role they assumed for all abandoned babies within the islands.

Now how to find this mermaid village? My father started asking locals about the predicted storm. He was curious why no one was worried. They told him that the Olympic rain shadow effect, caused by the Olympic Mountains, protected the San Juan Mountains from any heavy rainfall. He then asked about the threat of a Pacific hurricane. No one was concerned in this quaint little seaside tourist village.

The harbor was filled with boats. Every slip was taken with a houseboat or fishing boat. There were one or two fancy yachts that had signs for chartering on them. The relaxed vibe almost relaxed me, but the tension was building within my body. I thumbed through my notes and added the new information Brooke had provided. I had no Plan A, B, or C. Morgan was also tense. I could feel his concern and tension all the way up my spine. It was my father who was formulating a plan. He was calm and purposeful. The first thing he did was charter a boat for a diving tour. We would set sail in two hours.

We strolled the streets and saw signs for orca whale-watching tours, little shops selling tiny wooden totems, and an advertisement for the San Juan Sculpture Park. I felt bad for all the negative thoughts and beliefs we had been holding on to about my father. We had time before heading out to sea, so why not go to the park with him? Morgan read my thoughts as I looked at the picture. He wanted to share that experience with him, too. Who knew what we would encounter on the open water? Sculpture and metalwork were things we understood. They were solid and real. We may not have always understood his vision or why it was so important to him, but we knew it was. We showed him the sign for the park, and he wasn't interested.

Spencer chimed in, "Oh, that looks cool! We should check it out."

"Let's stay focused, kids. Open that notebook and let's figure out exactly where in these waterways we need to be looking."

We urged him to take a moment with us. We knew that deep down, he wanted to go. So he agreed. We rented some bikes and road the two miles to the park. We decided not to venture far into the park, just to take in a few of the sculptures. Each piece of art sat in an open area, juxtaposed with the beautiful nature surrounding us. Some pieces looked hard and isolating, and others flowed with the natural environment. It was difficult not to reach out and touch each one. There was one sculpture that called out to all of us. It was a diving orca whale made of wood and iron. Morgan touched the metal on the fin. He left his hand there for a moment, then suddenly clutched his head. I could feel the pain of an intense headache. My father rushed to his side, but Spencer got there first. He was proving to be an asset to our little squad.

"You okay?" He supported Morgan's swaying frame.

"Whoa—massive migraine."

He sat down on the ground for a moment. My stomach was queasy as I connected with his head pain. Another patron of the sculpture park came over to check on us. He was walking close behind us as we walked from sculpture to sculpture. I hadn't looked at him. I used the same strategy at all places where people didn't quite get personal space, even with groups. Mini-golf to museums, I avoided eye contact. I'm like the skilled waitress who pretends she has no peripheral vision and never sees you motion for a refill or the check. But now I got a good look at him. He was tall, fit, and wearing a clerical collar. This guy was a priest.

"Hello, are you folks okay? Can I be of some assistance?" He kneeled close to where Morgan sat on the ground. The priest had a satchel with some water and offered it to Morgan. I realized none of us had thought about drinking anything after our bike ride. He must have been super-dehydrated. We had checked our bags at a locker in town so we wouldn't be carrying anything other than the essentials. We had forgotten that water was one.

Spencer and our dad helped Morgan up. Morgan could stand on his own and looked like he was recovering. My father held out his hand to the priest.

"Thanks for your help. I'm Mitch and these are my kids, Morgan and Muriel, and their friend Spencer."

The priest shook my father's hand and nodded to us. "I'm Father Alexander. I assume you're visiting our little island archipelago." Morgan was giving off a weird vibe, and I couldn't really read it. It was suspicion. He hadn't been subscribing to my "ignore other humans in my space" philosophy; he had been paying attention. He had seen the priest watching us and walking a bit too close to our group. I figured he was just taking an interest in the new faces in town—just in case we might be available for conversion. Morgan was quick to respond in a terse, distrustful tone.

"Yes, visiting." He was about to say something else, but his phone buzzed. It was Brooke. "Excuse me." He stepped away to take the call, looking completely revived.

Spencer, my dad, and I continued the conversation with the priest. We chatted about the beautiful island and our plans to take in some sights. We didn't mention our upcoming dive. Spencer's call triggered my thoughts about the information Brooke had sent me. The abandoned babies at the parish. I tried to make a natural segue and ask about their role in adoptions, but it sounded more like a bizarre blurt.

"So our pilot said the orca pod may be missing its mother. It's so sad when babies don't have parents. Does that happen a lot around here?" My mouth was dry and I could have used a swig of that water Morgan had. I swallowed hard and made a weird gulp sound, which compounded the weirdness of my question. Morgan walked up as I made the weird noise. My dad just stared at me, wondering what I was doing. The priest scrutinized me carefully before answering me.

"It doesn't happen a lot. Why do you ask, my dear?" His glare was direct and dialing into my thoughts. He wasn't actually getting access to my mind but was tapping into my weakness—the direct question. I had never been able to evade or maneuver around the truth when someone asked me a direct question. There are at least a hundred horrifying and embarrassing stories of me saying things that no one wanted to know because a question compelled me to be truthful. I was about to answer when I felt my dad's hand on my shoulder.

"Nice to meet you, Father. We've got to be going."

His firm hand on my shoulder leading me away released the desire to utter a word. I smiled at Father Alexander and said, "Oh, no reason. Nice to meet you."

Morgan smiled at the priest, Spencer nodded at him, and we all hurried out of the sculpture park. We weren't sure why we were all so suddenly uncomfortable. We bought water at the gift shop, got on our bikes, and rode toward the dock. We grabbed our bags and checked in for our chartered boat. Dad might have to plan to never retire because we were spending all of our savings on this rescue mission. The sign over the entrance to the dock said, "Best Cold Water Diving." I wasn't excited about reading the "cold" part in the sign. I don't have a hardy constitution and don't like the cold. An invitation to a ski vacation was just another way of saying you didn't know me or didn't like me. I liked my hometown of San Diego. The moderate temperature year round, lack of rainfall, and practically no change in barometric pressure was my ideal weather situation. My recent cave event was the coldest I'd ever been there.

The sky on San Juan Island was changing. The predicted clouds were making their way into the sky, fluffy and dark. The wind was picking up, and my total inexperience with cold weather had led me to pack only a hoodie. Morgan looked at the clouds and reminded me of my mirror. He pointed to a map encased in a display on the dock near the tour boat. "Ask to see where we should dive. Look at the map." I looked around to see who might be watching. The coast was clear, and I set my intention on the map and asked to see where we should dive. In the mirror I saw the real landscape while I looked at the topography on the map. The Salish Sea is the waterway that flows between the islands. I saw Steller sea lions climbing up onto what looked like Brown Island. Then I saw a mermaid with dark coral-red hair and light-green and yellow scales swimming toward Lopez Island and a spot on the map that said Shark Reef Sanctuary. The mermaid paused in the water and it was like she was looking straight at me. Then she smiled. She *was* looking at me—startled, I dropped the mirror, and it broke.

Morgan and Spencer rushed over to me. "What happened?"

We bent down to pick up the fractured pieces, but they turned into grains of sand as we touched them. Spencer let some of the grains run through his fingers. "Whoa!"

"Why didn't this come with a warning or better instructions?" I groused. The wind picked up the remains of the mirror sand and dropped them into the sea. The clouds moved in stronger and the wind whipped loudly, sending us a clear message that a storm was brewing. Dad motioned for us to join him at the edge of the dock where our gear was being loaded. We had wet suits and other dive gear. Luckily for us, this wouldn't be our first underwater rodeo. When we were ten, we took a two-week class during the summer. We were both hoping that it was true about sensory memory—our muscles and cells would remember how to breathe and dive safely. Spencer was an avid diver, so I looked to him for some tips. My confidence wasn't high as I started to remember that my participation that summer wasn't actually considered participation. I watched as the other kids learned how to use the equipment in the YMCA pool. I would sit on the side and wave at Morgan as he blew bubbles. Another strike against the power of the introvert. Skills—I was lacking skills.

I told Morgan what I had seen. The map and mirror showed the entire San Juan Archipelago, which not only included US San Juan Islands, but also the Canadian Gulf Islands. There were rocks, lagoons, caves, and 450 islands that were part of a submerged mountain chain. So many nooks and crannies for us to search, but we had a starting point: Lopez Island. I looked up at the sky: the air was strange and thick.

The captain informed us about all his boat offered. He had sonar, plenty of room for tanks, and several kayaks if we decided that we wanted to do that instead while we were by the islands. We boarded the boat and headed out into the crystal-blue water. I told my dad about the mirror's fate and where we should go. He told the captain we wanted to start near Brown Island and work our way toward Lopez Island. He thought the water would be better for diving by Brown Island, so he was happy to start there, since it was very close to the harbor.

We put our gear on and were in the water within minutes. The water was chilly, but my wetsuit protected me from the extreme cold that I was expecting. I knew we were looking for my mother and anything that would lead to her, but I was mesmerized by what lay just beneath the surface. Red and purple sea urchins, crimson anemones with silky-looking tentacles, orange-yellow flowing cup corals, and sponges covered the rocks and sea floor. The four of us swam together, and Morgan communicated with me with our newfound twin mind connection. I was calm and comforted below the surface of the sea. The gear was easy to use, and my swimming was effortless with the addition of the fins. I smiled and laughed as I realized the underwater world wasn't silent for us. We heard each other and the clicks and songs and squeaks of the other animals beneath the surface.

My father tried to use what little sign language he knew to

communicate. We were looking for a cave or something that looked like the start of the construction that was in the mirror image during the seaplane ride. There were craggy rocks, shallow depressions, erosion, and plenty of fish swimming by, but nothing that resembled the image from the mirror. I felt something brush up against me. A sweet-faced harbor porpoise was nudging me. It was much smaller and slimmer than the dolphins that had trapped my mother in the cove. It swam playfully between Morgan and me, then swam near my father. He looked like he wanted us to follow him, so we did.

I knew of these little guys from researching the sea life of the Puget Sound area while we flew from San Diego. They had been meeting a tragic fate at the hands of the beloved orca pods people came here to see. Some orcas were killing them for play or sport, not for food, since orcas eat Chinook salmon. The orcas and harbor porpoises don't even compete for food. They'd literally play with these well-intentioned porpoises to death. It was just another reminder that everything on this planet above or below the sea might have its own unknown agenda.

We swam away from the boat, closer toward the shoreline of San Juan Island. A portly friend joined the porpoise, and they nodded their noses and swam to the surface. Morgan and my dad motioned that we should follow. When we reached the surface, everything topside had changed. The sky was black, and the sea was thrashing. The boat swayed violently from side to side. The water below the surface was changing. The currents swirled, and the anemones were having trouble staying positioned on the rocks. Our location between the two land masses of San Juan Island and Brown Island shielded us from the intensity of the storm for now. It was building out deeper, ready to bring in enormous waves crashing on land. The captain urged us to get in the boat. Morgan wasn't ready to give up the search just yet, though. He had the comb with him. Spencer swam back toward the boat and looked back at us. He motioned for us to follow.

"Muriel, I'll try to reach some sand near the erosion at the edge of the rocks." Morgan swam back down under the surface. The harbor porpoise swam with him. The captain shouted at us. He thought if he used the comb the way Calliope told him by combing the sand and sea together, we could fast track my mom's location and bring her home.

"Where is he going? We've got to get back to shore. This storm's really happened."

The captain's voice was hard to hear over the scream of the wind and waves. He seemed amazed the sea had mustered up the guts to bring a Pacific hurricane all the way to their historically protected spot of the earth. The waterways of the strait of Georgia and the strait of Juan de Fuca had intense currents, but the topography of the region shielded them. There hadn't been a serious Pacific hurricane since tropical cyclone Patsy in 1959. The captain helped my father on board as he talked. I dove back down to help Morgan.

Morgan reached a small mount with coral and sea urchins attached. It had a sloping side with its own collection of sand before it dropped off into a deep trench, like a little mini-beach for the residents of that habitat. Something was amiss in the little ocean community. A European green crab and a red rock crab were battling for turf. The green crab was an invasive species. It had its picture plastered all over town. They had signs near the dock that resembled wanted posters— wanted dead or alive for crimes against the environment of local crabs. Morgan found a spot free of creatures and pulled the comb out of his dive belt. He ran it through the sand several times and waited. The storm above raged, and the sands below swirled upwards revealing the grains' variety of colors—amber, copper, and cocoa mixed with the tan bits of earth and shell. The sand was clouding the water. I moved in closer to Morgan and urged him to get back up to the surface, but he was waiting for the promised help. He thought he might need to call out. I could hear his call loudly. My father looked over the side of the swaying boat trying to see us and was considering jumping back in the water.

The captain grabbed my father and restrained him. "Help us! We need to find our mother. Help us find her." Morgan and I locked hopeful eyes.

The porpoises swam close to each of us. The portly one swam between Morgan's and my gaze. He knocked at my tank. I remembered my actual skill level with diving and waved my hands in front of me, hoping to get him to leave me alone. The other slender porpoise tugged at Morgan's dive belt and almost knocked the comb out of his hands.

The water above us was suddenly unstable. The boat capsized. My father and the captain were dumped into the water. My father thrashed about, and the captain floated aimlessly. Our once crystal-clear Samish Sea was murky and devoid of the welcoming colors that greeted us when we first submerged. The lack of light from the sky created a dim and gloomy current carrying uprooted creatures, rocks, and shells. The porpoises stayed close to us. The crabs were long gone. Neither species wanted any part of this turf war; they were looking for shelter.

A twinkling off in the distance beyond the coastline appeared as if there were an underwater constellation of shimmering stars. The glittery mass moved closer to us, providing light in our darkened surroundings. Before I could process that my dad was in the water and might need help and that the captain was most likely unconscious, my eyes focused on the glistening scaled bodies of bejeweled mermaids. There were ten of them, all youthful and beautiful. Their facial features varied, with some looking more human than others. Their eyes were like my mother's near the cove—dark, with no perceptible whites, like a seal's eye. An eleventh mermaid appeared from the center of the group. Her eyes were clear and human. I recognized her. It was Stella, the mermaid who had rescued Spencer. I had a twinge of jealousy when I thought about the raven-haired beauty holding Spencer in her arms. She looked the same, except now she wore a bodice of golden seashells, pearls, and starfish, which resembled the braided adornments in her flowing hair.

My dad saw the congregation of mermaids and stopped treading water, shocked by his first sighting of what type of creature he had been married to for all of these years. Debris from the boat and the storm reaching the unconscious captain shifted his attention. He swam toward him and surfaced with the captain, hoping they would both get oxygen. He clung to a kayak that had broken free from the boat. Spencer was also clinging to a kayak and swam to my dad to link them.

Below the surface, the population continued to increase. Several harbor porpoises joined our earlier friends, and they created a barrier between Morgan and the dead-eyed sea beauties. Up from the inky depths emerged the gigantic, bulbous reddish-brown head of the giant Pacific octopus. Its enormous tentacles spread out quickly in the water, revealing the two rows of white suckers beneath each of its eight reaching body parts. It appeared behind Morgan and scooped him up, enveloping his wetsuit. The porpoises turned to aid Morgan, and I swam toward my father, trying to reach one of his legs to get his attention. Morgan screamed in my mind. I could feel his moment of panic, but then courage and bravery when he shouted: *"Get out of the water, Muriel. Get out of the water."*

There must have been a cavern that we hadn't seen. The entrance we had been looking for must have been blocked by this burnished beast. Suddenly, Stella spoke to me. I could hear her words clearly. We could all communicate. "Listen to your brother. We have no use for you."

The storm waters and current changed swiftly. A rush of water rose and headed toward the shore. The boat was pushed closer to Brown Island. My father had the captain positioned on the side of the kayak. Spencer reached them. The captain was breathing but unconscious. My dad tried to see under the waves, but the briny swell was blinding him without his facemask. He couldn't see what was happening below.

Morgan pleaded with Stella. "We just want to find our mother!" The octopus swam away with Morgan. I tried to swim after him. My porpoise friends tried to assist me by letting me hang on to them, increasing my speed.

Stella sweetened her voice when she started speaking to Morgan. "Morgan, your mother is not even in these waters. She has been returned to her homeland. You will not find her here. We can reunite you, though."

I had had it. I was close to the octopus. My deep well of misplaced rage had been filling up as this underwater vixen sweet-talked my brother. First she mesmerized Spencer, and now she was trying to abduct my brother just like that other merman thing did with my mom. My anger was electrically charged, and I could feel the heat coming from my belly and warming my whole body. The storm in the sea swept through, and a blast of uprooted animals glided through the group of mermaids. Sea horses and coral flew into their faces and bodies. I snatched a large, jagged shell and struck the arm of the octopus. His blue blood trickled into the water. He released my brother for a moment. A porpoise drew near to aid Morgan, but the octopus released his inky toxin into the water and the porpoise withdrew.

The octopus reclaimed his hold on my brother. The toxin filled the water around me, clouding my vision. My helplessness filled me with even more anger pulsing through every nerve fiber in my body. I could hear Stella and the direction of her voice. "There is nothing you can do. Heed your brother's warning."

The mermaids were humming or chanting something, sounding like some kind of underwater Gregorian chorus. I remembered my father above me and the advice he would give me in this situation. I thought about my mother stroking my hair and telling me how to channel all the energy I'd struggled with my whole life. I had not lost my faith, even in the midst of the myriad of contradictions between what I had learned and what I now knew. I sent a prayer up to the heavens: "Help me."

A surge of energy radiated out of my body with a buzzing electrical current, much like an eel. I released two rapid bursts of energy, which traveled through the water at everything I couldn't see. The electricity in the water shocked and controlled every creature within its range. The octopus, with its eight arms, three hearts, and nine brains, was now out of this fight. My brother was free, but he too received the blast. The inky water cleared as he floated closer to the mermaids. He clutched the comb in his hand. It glowed with a gentle light. I intercepted his floating body and swam him toward the surface, where my dad and Spencer struggled with the kayaks. The surface crested and curled. Waves knocked into the kayaks, pushing us all closer to San Juan Island. Morgan looked strange. The shock wasn't wearing off. I dumped my tank and his so we could maneuver on the kayak.

Stella projected her voice from the ocean floor. "We're waiting for you, Morgan." The mermaids began their chants and humming.

Morgan pleaded with us. "We need to get to the shore." Morgan's voice was raspy, and his skin was pale.

We were very close to the shore, but we were battling the beginning of the hurricane-force winds. We struggled, but we made the edge of the coastline and dug in. My father grabbed the captain first. People were on the shore acting as rescuers, helping anyone they saw in or near the water. Several men rushed down the sloping beach and helped us to safety. Anything not nailed down was attempting to take flight. The captain was transported to the hospital, and we were shuttled to a designated emergency shelter.

Even though the residents of Friday Harbor hadn't been overly concerned with the threat of the storm, the government officials had created contingency plans for preparedness. When our shuttle ride was over, we found ourselves at the entrance to the local Catholic church. It looked like this was the hub they had chosen for tourists. The tiny island had only a few places where they could house extra people; luckily, we weren't in the height of tourist season. There were only about twenty people inside the church. Pews had been set up like cots, there was a medical crew, and a table was covered with food and water. A firefighter was helping us find our place and recommended that we get checked out by the medical team. I was sure that I would catch pneumonia, since this was the second time I had been wrapped in emergency blankets to warm up from the icy unforgiving water. I was surprised that I didn't feel sick, but I was waiting for it. It was Morgan who looked worn out and pale. I felt guilty about my unexpected underwater electrical blast. I didn't think about him being in the path, but I also didn't know that I was going to be able to do that, so I guess I could forgive myself. I was in a church, after all. As I continued to ruminate, I saw Father Alexander walk out of the confessional. We locked eyes, and he smiled.

Spencer noticed him, too. "Hey, Muri—look who's here."

He walked straight for our group. The firefighter introduced us to him. "This is Father Lutey. He's in charge of the entire San Juan Islands parish. He'll help you with whatever you need."

My heart dropped to my stomach. None of us missed the name. Spencer blurted, "Lutey!"

The priest spoke up. "Yes, thank you for the introduction, Walter. I already met this lovely family earlier today."

Walter saw that he was needed closer to the medic crew and nodded at all of us. "Okay, good. Now don't forget, I think you should get checked out. Right over there." He walked off in the direction of a woman who had fainted. The wind thrashed against the building. The eye of the storm was supposed to miss the San Juan Archipelago; we were experiencing just a fraction of what part of the mainland farther south might experience.

My father looked at the priest with suspicion. "I thought you were Father Alexander."

The priest smiled warmly. "Some parishioners still feel like they need to follow the old ways and refer to us by our last name. I feel like we're a bit more modern here. I always introduce myself by my first name."

"So you're Father Alexander Lutey?" I asked, almost in a whisper.

"Yes, that's correct." He looked at Morgan. "He's not looking well." Morgan chose to lie down on the pew. "Is he still suffering from the migraine?"

My father didn't respond. Instead, he asked another question regarding the name. I could feel Morgan's emotions getting fuzzy, and the thoughts he was sharing with me were unclear. He had the humming of the mermaid's song in his mind.

"That's an unusual last name. Where does it come from?"

My dad feigned ignorance over the origin of his own name. Father Alexander Lutey had a weird glint in his eye and lowered his voice. "Scotland. Your family comes from Scotland."

My dad's eyes widened. Now my heart was pounding loudly in my ears—but was it my heart I was hearing? No, it was Morgan's. His breathing was rapid, his pulse racing. His body started to convulse. I called out to the medics. Spencer ran toward Walter and shouted, "We need help over here!"

I tried to stabilize Morgan's body, but his arms were twitching. My dad came to his side and opened his mouth. I think he was going to try and grab his tongue so he didn't swallow it, but Walter and a medic were now in charge of my brother's care. They looked in his eyes, which were showing only the whites. They stabilized his body and took his vitals, and then put an extra blanket on him and gave him some oxygen. His body stopped convulsing, and his breathing became less erratic. He seemed to be returning to us. Walter helped him sit up, while the other medic asked him questions to assess his brain function.

"I think he should be taken to the hospital once the storm passes," the medic said.

"What's happening to him? Is it hypothermia?" my dad queried the medic and looked at the readings on the blood pressure cuff.

"Not sure. He seems okay now. Let's just get him checked out again. Keep an eye on him. Has he eaten?"

I realized we hadn't eaten. We hadn't really had anything since our coffee breakfast at the airport this morning. I was able to rationalize this situation with his desperate need for a bagel or soup. It couldn't have anything to do with octopuses, mermaids, or electrical currents. My vote was extreme low blood sugar. I didn't care what the name was of this kooky priest, I was going to get my brother a sandwich or something.

I kissed Morgan on the cheek and rushed over to the refreshment table. I started stacking everything I could see that was a complex carbohydrate, then realized he probably needed protein, too. I could feel people's eyes on me as I grabbed things at a frenetic pace. I used my "I'm ignoring you, I have no peripheral vision" technique to evade their awkward glances that may have suggested I limit the number of cheese sticks I had on my plate. I juggled my mix of goodies and beverages and made it back to my father and the Father, who looked to be having a heated debate. I wasn't able to avoid the looks of the gawkers in this situation, since I looked around to see who was watching. The priest also became aware of the eyes on all of us. Spencer was trying to play referee but wasn't having any luck.

"Why don't you folks join me in my office where we can chat in private?" Father Lutey guided all four of us into another, more secluded section of the church. Morgan drank some soda and munched on a cheese stick. I looked at him, pleased with myself that I thought of bringing a cheese stick. He smiled at me as I thought this. The color was slowly coming back to his face. I was surprised he was able to walk after what his body had just been through. Spencer juggled the plate of food and whatever possessions we had left. Waterproof bags had been his idea, and we were grateful.

The priest's office was sufficiently decorated in religious artifacts, but also had its fair share of nautical-themed items. There were several pictures of the Father on a research boat, and also pictures of him dressed in a Navy uniform with other cadets. He had a certificate from some course he took through the University of Washington at something called the Friday Harbor Lab. It looked like being on the water was part of his regular life. That made sense, since he would have to travel between all of the tiny islands to meet with parishioners who might be in need. I looked at his pictures more closely—maybe there was a family resemblance. As soon as the door was shut behind us, my father charged at the priest aggressively and pinned him against the wall. Morgan and I held our breath in anticipation of what would come next. Spencer pulled my dad off the priest. We'd never seen our dad in action like this. We knew that he had gotten into a fight with Uncle Nohea and that Mom had mentioned that in his youth he could be a bit of a hothead. Yet this was extreme even for him. The priest was considerably older than my father, so it was hard to watch.

"Tell me, old man. What the hell is going on?"

Father Lutey didn't flinch. His military training was evident by his resolve. He brushed Dad off, then stood as tall as he could, creating a physical distance of confidence between him and my dad. He definitely wasn't cornered or afraid.

"Relax. Take a seat. I'll answer anything you want to know. No need for brute force." This admonishment brought my father to his senses, and he released the priest while trying to gain his composure. My father stayed standing, but I sat down.

"What do you know about what's been going on with our family?"

Father Lutey went behind his desk and sat down in a big comfortable chair. He had a pitcher of water on the desk and a few glasses. He poured himself a glass and offered us some. We declined. The wind outside howled, but it seemed farther in the distance now, instead of right on top of the church.

"We do very special work in this parish." Father Lutey looked at me when he said this. "I know you asked about orphaned babies earlier. We receive, find, and adopt out babies every few years. It's a very special thing when it happens."

Morgan spoke up. "We know our mother was brought to this parish."

The priest nodded. "Yes, I know your mother's story. I'd actually forgotten about it but was recently reminded by a student at the Friday Harbor Laboratory." He pointed to the certification that I saw earlier. "The lab is part of the University of Washington. Researchers and students come from all over the world to study here. Our environment has many unique species—for example, the giant Pacific octopus."

My father stood up again and started to pace. "Just get to the point. Enough of the history of Friday Harbor." He slammed his fist down on the desk. "My wife is missing, and we need to find her."

Apparently when they were talking earlier, Father Lutey had been giving my father a history lesson about how he and the Lutey clan had ended up in Friday Harbor. He had been discussing at length the particular flora and fauna of the Pacific Northwest. The Luteys made their way to the new world from Scotland by way of Canada. They eventually moved further south to the United States. There was also another family group named Pellar that was still in Scotland, but were more travelers than the Luteys, and they could be found in Ireland, Australia, South America, and Asia. He said they were all charged with important work and were keeping the delicate ecosystem in balance. This is when we saw their discussion get heated by the pews.

"Yes, I understand you want to find your wife. Let me be clear. That will not happen on this trip to Friday Harbor." My father looked like he was going to push the priest over in his comfy chair. I got up to stand between them.

"Please, just tell us what you know about our mother!" I pleaded, and kept my father from lunging at the priest. I glanced over at Morgan, who still looked slightly dazed. The priest looked at the door to the hall and got up, walking carefully around my father. He locked the door and returned to his seat, took a sip of water, and began to speak in a quiet tone.

"I'll be direct, since that seems to be what is required in this situation. As you already know, your mother is a mermaid." As the priest spoke, I let the breath out that I had been holding and returned to my seat. No convincing or pleading for the truth needed to be done. The priest pointed to my notebook.

"You may want to take notes, since I won't have the opportunity to be with you wherever this may lead you." I thumbed through my notebook. I then offered Morgan a sip of water as we waited for the priest to continue. My father also grabbed a chair.

"Sometimes, very rarely, we find infant mermaids trapped in nets or caught in currents that are led to our shores. We take them in and place them with a good family and educate them in our ways. They know nothing of what their lives would have been in the sea or who their parents are. Most go on to lead exceptional lives." I already had issues with this relocation plan that he was describing, but I was focused on what my mother's story was.

"And our mother?" Morgan was quick to respond before I could get my thought out.

"Your mother was brought to us for safe keeping." He shuffled through a desk drawer searching for a picture.

"Who brought her? The fisherman?" my father asked.

"Yes, ultimately the story was of a fisherman bringing her here, but he was actually part of our clergy who was out fishing that day. Your mother was handed to him by her mother—your grandmother—the most beautiful blonde woman he had ever seen, with the tail of a sea creature. His vow of chastity helped him keep his wits about him. He said he would have followed her into the depths of the ocean if she had asked, but he kept praying the entire time he was with her, and thankfully she had another request. She asked him to take her baby and have her go far away from these shores. She told him that she was a very special little girl, and there was a prophecy about her and this child. Even though it broke her heart—they must be separated. The priest on the boat was a believer in all the old texts and stories. He had thought that every story of old had a bit of truth to it. It was just finding the truth—and there she swam in front of him."

Father Lutey then continued with a story about the most infamous biblical believers in mermaids—the Assyrians. They believed in a goddess by the name of Atargatis; the Romans called her Dea Syriae. The Sumerians and Babylonians also had names for this sea goddess. The Ancient Philistines could also be counted as those with a god resembling a merman—Dagon. In the bible, Samson's last act was to destroy the Philistine temple of Dagon. Also of great interest to the fisherman priest was the comparison between Noah's flood in Genesis of the bible and the Sumerian Gilgamesh poems from the 27th century BC, which also had a universal flood. In fact, there seemed to be a universal flood story within all ancient cultures that was brought on by man's wickedness.

The truth as told by this mermaid giving up her child was the story he had been waiting for his whole life. This mermaid was no demon, nor was she pretending to be a god. She was merely a mother and servant, just like he was. Her people had their own creation story and savior story. They coexisted in very similar realities with rules and order. Their creator sounded exactly like his creator. Just as on land, there were zealots of their beliefs in her world, but they had great powers, since they were descended from the angels as well as Adam and Eve. They believed that the wickedness of man would eventually lead to the destruction of the earth again, so that man should be minimized and kept in check.

I interrupted the priest's mermaid theology lesson. I wanted to know more about why we wouldn't be able to rescue my mother here in Friday Harbor.

"Okay, so we get it. Mermaids are real. People have believed forever. Now we're getting my mom back today. How are we doing that?"

Father Lutey, our newfound cousin, stood up and walked over to

Morgan, who was still looking under the weather. "You have a bigger concern right now. Your mother is gone. You still might be able to save your brother."

This shocked my father into attention. He had glazed over a bit with the mermaid history lesson. "What are you talking about?" He walked over to Morgan as if to shield him from the words that might be coming next.

"Your son is a triton, and the third merperson in the prophecy. He's already started changing."

Morgan and I spoke in unison. "Not happening. I don't think so. We are not turning into mer-people."

We echoed this sentiment in true twin style, beginning and ending our sentences at the same time. We were in sync. Our brains were firing with all sorts of thoughts about our family, about the ocean, and what we could do to stop what this priest was trying to make seem like fate. One thing our parents had always agreed upon and were fierce about communicating was that we made our fates. Our future and destiny were our own.

I had a moment of doubt. My mother's destiny did resemble one that she wasn't guiding at all. First she was given up by her mother, then raised by strangers never knowing her true identity, then she married my dad—did she have to do that? Was she under the Lutey spell? Would she have rather married someone else, or no one at all? As my thoughts raced the priest broke through the thought frenzy.

"Muriel. It is just Morgan that is changing."

When he said this, my hands went cold. The blood drained from my face and tears started streaming down my cheeks. I began to hyperventilate. I could feel Morgan's fear rising up in his body. He knew that he was changing. What the priest said felt true. He knew something had changed when he was facing the mermaids and they were calling to him. So here we were back again to the beginning. The differences—the idea that DNA was real. We had shared a womb, but we were two very separate and different little embryos evolving into unique people. I was a high-strung, introverted girl that would have been "given a pass" if I had been a boy. My behaviors would have been acceptable if they had been exhibited by a male wild child—I would have almost been admired as they tried to tame me without truly expecting success. Instead I was judged as having too much energy, being too emotional, too everything. Why was I being excluded from this as well? I suppressed my self-obsessed monkey brain and tried to slow it down. This was about Morgan. This was about Mom.

My dad looked at the priest. "What the hell are you talking about?"

Father Lutey touched Morgan's pulse on his wrist and looked in his eyes. He felt behind Morgan's right ear. Morgan winced, then felt behind his ear as well.

"Gills. They're coming in." My father, Spencer, and I rushed to look behind Morgan's ear, but he blocked it.

"No. Listen up. This is not happening. He's deflecting. He still hasn't told us how to find Mom. That is why we are here. So, priest—spill it. Where is my mother!"

"Your mother is most likely in the area of her namesake, the loreley. It's located on the right bank of the Rhine River. Or she has already made it back to meet her sisters the selkies and her brothers the blue men of the Muir in the Minch Channel off the coast of Northern Scotland."

I looked at Morgan, and his skin had a mild blue-gray cast to it as if he were still very, very cold.

"We were told that she was returning to her homeland," Spencer retorted.

"That is her homeland. She wasn't born in these waters. Her mother traveled here with her."

There was a knock on the door to his office as he finished his words. My father sank into a chair, defeated. Father Lutey moved to the door to unlock and open it. He opened it partially. There was another member of the clergy outside the door.

"Are you alright, Father? May I be of any assistance? The storm has passed on from the island and people are free to return to their hotels." The clergyman tried to get a peek inside the room, trying to ascertain the welfare of the priest who had been missing from view for quite some time during an emergency situation. Father Lutey was pleased by the intrusion.

"Perfect, Michael—is everything in order out there?" He welcomed Michael into the office. He sized us up and could surmise there were high emotions in the room.

"Yes, everything is being handled out there. How may I assist you here?" He looked long and hard at my father, who was now mumbling to himself.

"Let me introduce you to some of my newfound kin—Mitch, Muriel, Morgan, and their good friend Spencer. They're south coast Luteys from San Diego. Weren't you based in San Diego at one time?" Michael nodded yes to the question and motioned hello but did not move to shake hands or greet us in any physical way. He stayed close to the door, still not trusting the situation. He looked very athletic and took up a lot of space with his stance. His complexion looked naturally tan. Father Lutey could see that he was uneasy and suspicious of the group. He tried to break the ice.

"So this is their first time on the island. I met them earlier at the sculpture garden. You like that place, don't you?"

"Yes. I like that place. All M names, huh? Interesting family choice," Michael commented with a slight Spanish accent. "Last year you worked very closely with a student researcher from the Friday Harbor Lab. The one that ended up taking a few files that were not his...."

Father Lutey gave Michael the okay to let him know it was alright to discuss whatever this unpleasant topic was. "Yes, Michael. Why do you ask about him?" It was clear Michael didn't want to go into the story. "Michael, it's not your fault. I was deceived by him as well. Please just tell them about it. I think they may know something about him." This comment interested Michael.

"Colin is his name. He came from Scotland and was studying an effect known as rainbow sea spray. There's an area near the shark sanctuary that encounters a lot of this optical illusion. Anyway, he befriended us all. I'm a regular volunteer at the lab in my free time, because when I was in the military I helped train dolphins and sea lions."

We knew a lot about this military program that Michael mentioned. Brooke, like a lot of her classmates, had spent the first part of the year protesting. They protested everything from things on campus to the use of plastics, random political stuff, GMO labeling, free trade, and zero waste—whatever was the latest horrible thing happening. Logically they were also savvy about what was going on in our own backyard. One day her boycott team got wind of what was going on at the military base with the dolphins, and that was that. She had a new crusade that we were all informed about. This protest didn't get further than her exhaustive research, because it was military. They weren't about to let a bunch of teenagers wreak havoc on government property.

The marine mammal program, which included dolphins and sea lions, was started in the 1960s and was very mysterious. The dolphins were utilized in combat during the Vietnam and Iraq Wars. The animals were grouped into five marine mammal teams. Three teams were trained to hunt sea mines. One was a combo of dolphins and sea lions that protected areas from unauthorized human swimmers. The last team was all sea lions trained for object recovery, including open-water victims. The Navy listed dozens of other sea creatures used during their programs with less noted success—many varieties of whales, dolphins, seals, birds, and even sharks. I was instantly judging Michael because he participated with their training.

My father interrupted Michael. "Colin? You know him? Where can we find him?" Michael was irritated that he was interrupted. He didn't seem like someone with much patience—an unlikely character for the clergy.

"He was spotted in town before the storm started," he responded.

The priest dismissed Michael with a simple, "Thank you, I'll be with everyone shortly." Michael nodded and quickly excused himself.

Father Lutey directed his comment to me. "He'll know by now that Morgan is chosen. He was using the files to search for the other children that had been placed from our parish. He suspected the third member of the prophecy would come from that group." I wondered why he was talking directly to me, sidelining the rest of the group.

Morgan could hear my thoughts and responded, *"I still don't trust this guy, Muri. Let's get out of here. I don't care what he says. I'm not turning into a merman. Let's stay focused on Mom."* Morgan moved toward the door and unlocked it. He looked at Spencer and my dad.

"Let's go." He was out the door and I was right behind him.

Our cousin the priest then called out to me. "Muriel. Keep him away from the water." I was regretting leaving. There were so many questions I had about everything. I wanted to know the real history of the curse and what it meant for us. How many Luteys had been taken by the sea? I wanted to know how to save Morgan, if he truly was changing. Once we got outside the church, we could see that some of the infrastructure was damaged. Street signs were knocked down, trees were uprooted, and the sky was still dark and was now raining. Morgan checked his phone to see if flights were being re-routed or if they were still landing.

"Let's head back to San Diego and regroup. Maybe Scotland is next?" Morgan campaigned for a quick pack-up and vanish. I pushed the same thought into his mind that Spencer spoke: *"What about Colin? If he's here, don't we need to find him?"* I took a deep breath and told them what I felt: "I don't know if Colin is here, but I don't believe that Mom isn't. We keep hearing that she's gone—but I feel it. She's nearby. It's more than a gut feeling—it's a knowing. We need to keep looking for her."

My dad and Morgan hesitated for a moment, then Spencer proclaimed, "Muriel, I'll keep looking with you."

My dad looked at Morgan and could see him ailing and the fear in his eyes. "I'll stay with Morgan, and we'll spend one more day looking for your mother, but let's forget about Colin. He isn't worth our time."

When we had landed on San Juan Island, we had gotten right to business with no long-term thinking about our plans. We didn't have a hotel room booked or any idea what was coming next. The storm had the town in disarray. The ferry was up and running, and tourists were either trying to recapture what they hoped would be a vacation or fleeing the island. We thought this mass exodus would open up a couple of rooms in one of the rentals or bed and breakfasts on the island. We debated about where we would go next. Should we check out the Friday Harbor Lab area, or should we move closer to the shark sanctuary?

We agreed step one was to find a place to spend the night. We picked an inn within walking distance of the ferry terminal. The contemporary two-story inn had views from every angle of the property. If we were tourists wanting to stay put, we would have been able to watch orcas while sipping hot cocoa from our balcony. My brother stood on the balcony, staring out at the water. I let him have his private moment, and I cracked open my notebook.

Father Lutey had mentioned lots of weird new information, and I wasn't sure how much was relevant to what we were doing. He hadn't mentioned anything about sirens. I still couldn't figure out how they fit into the mermaid world or what exactly Colin was. It was mentioned that he was a "believer" and that he was part of a group that searched for lost members of the nephilim. Were there other types of half-human creatures living among us? I wondered what they turned into. Were they all merpeople? Were they sick and suffering like my mother was because she didn't know her true identity? Were we truly divided into two groups, the humans on land and whatever lay beneath the ocean? I pulled open the old texts and started to cross-reference my information. Some of the titles mentioned selkies, tritons, and the blue men of the Muir. They were all basically just types of related mer-people. I decided to take a knee and pray. I prayed harder than I ever had for answers.

My father touched me on the shoulder. "Is it helping?"

I stood up. It was at least helping me feel a bit calmer. My dad picked a spot next to the book on the bed and started thumbing through it as well.

"Who would have thought that your Uncle Nohea was actually right about what he saw out there on the open water?" A piece of paper fell out of one of the books while my dad was looking through the pages. I picked it up. It was the story of the Lutey curse—or, as it was written on this paper, Lutey's blessing. In this account, our ancestor Lutey was given three wishes for helping a mermaid. He chose to be able to break evil spells, have the power to get others to do good deeds, and that these blessings would pass on to his family forever. Then it told how the mermaid who gave him these wishes tried to take him underwater and drown him, but he used his iron knife to ward off the attempt. She came back for him years later, and he didn't fight when she took him to the sea. The blessing stayed with the family, but the curse or price of dealing with this mermaid was death by sea for a descendant every nine years—forever. There was one detail that I noticed I had also written in my notebook and circled. Iron. I showed it to my dad.

"What do you think we're dealing with here, Dad? Do you think we're going to need a weapon of some kind to protect Morgan? I brought the iron necklace." I pulled it out of my bag and my dad examined it.

"I'm not sure what you could do with it, Muri."

I decided to put it on.

"Maybe it will act like garlic to a vampire—come give me a hug and we'll see," Morgan said sarcastically. I frowned and didn't move.

There was a knock at the door. Spencer looked through the

peephole and opened it. It was pizza delivery. Spencer had suggested we have one solid meal together before we went our separate ways. Even though we had many favorite meals, all cooked by my mother, pizza was our family nourishment—our Dad meal. When anything was wrong or we needed it to be easy, pizza was there for us. We sat in silence eating slice after slice until it was all gone and there was nothing left keeping us together. I needed to go look for my mother, leaving the Lutey men behind.

I called my Uncle Nohea. "Can you call in any favors? We need the use of a boat with serious sonar and underwater surveillance ability."

He told me he had a contact and to meet them by the dock. I filled everyone in, and Spencer and I got ready to go. I hugged my dad and I hugged my brother. His skin was cold and slightly scaly. Spencer hugged my brother, then for some reason he hugged me. His hug lasted a bit longer than expected. I didn't pull away, even though I wasn't a big hugger. The non-hugging fell into my body space philosophy. There was a perfectly good invisible box that was around each of us and it should be respected at all times. The only exception to the rule was family, but I felt safe and protected in his arms and didn't want to pull away. I tried to rationalize it. I thought I had once read an article about male pheromones being calming if you were stressed out. Any male pheromones, not just someone you liked. I'm pretty sure I read that somewhere.

Morgan eavesdropped on my thoughts. *"I knew you had a thing for him, sis."*

I blushed and pulled away from Spencer and looked out onto the balcony. I had a sudden pang of fear. I wasn't about to lose my brother to the sea—or anything else, for that matter. I needed to find the right weapon to keep him safe. I didn't think this necklace would cut it. Something had happened underwater. I had harnessed some kind of power. I needed to see if I could reproduce it.

My dad pointed to Morgan, who was back on the balcony. "We

have a complication. Something is going on with Morgan. He might be...." My father had trouble getting the words out. He took a deep breath and continued, "Morgan might be transforming. Don't be gone too long." Morgan was looking paler and blueish.

"I'm glad you're staying here. I'm going to locate Mom or at least find that mermaid city I saw in the mirror. Someone will be able to help us." As I was leaving, I had an idea. "Morgan, you can call Calliope. Maybe she's here already. She was frequently lurking around when Colin was making his plans. I have a feeling she's a fly on the wall in here."

"Why me?" He looked puzzled.

I cast my eyes downward. I really did know something that they didn't. "You were always the one who called her," I said.

"What are you talking about? She was in the forest with you and in your dreams," he responded.

I knew what he was saying wasn't true. There was no logic to it, but I knew. I sensed her and knew her thoughts. "She was in the forest that day to test me, but once you entered her space, she knew that it was you that she was supposed to guide."

Morgan called out to test the theory: "Calliope." She appeared, and everyone in the room could see her. My father gripped a chair as he tried to maintain his balance from the surprise. We had told him every detail about our experience with the sirens, Colin, and Mom, but he was still processing. I could feel that it frightened him.

Once he was solid on his feet, he pushed Morgan and myself behind him. "Which demon are you?"

Calliope laughed, as she often did when we were engaging frightened or serious emotions. She was short on empathy for the human race. "I am no demon, sir. I am merely someone slightly different from you."

Morgan pushed past my dad. He seemed tired and winded. "Have you been here all along?"

Calliope found a comfortable place to sit and fluffed up part of her feathers. She was sitting near the books and thumbed through one of them. She was very matter of fact when she responded to Morgan.

"Yes, I'm like the little angel sitting on your shoulder. I'm with you now until you transition into the briny depths. I see you used the comb."

"You said it would bring help!" I shouted at her.

My father was still insistent that this was some sort of demon. He crossed himself and started saying a prayer, hoping to protect us. Calliope could see his antics and she was amused. "You can genuflect and cross yourself all you want; it's not going to change anything." She again giggled. I didn't like the way she was mocking us or the way she was disrespecting my father and his faith. I leapt out toward her, about to make feathers fly, but Spencer stepped in and blocked my path. He tried to keep me safe from what the wrath of this siren might be. Calliope had taken up a battle stance when I lunged.

Morgan spoke up. "So what is the truth? Just be honest with us. Tell me the truth." Morgan mustered up all of his strength and commanded a response.

Calliope smiled. "I was wondering if you Luteys would ever figure it out. I'm compelled to answer you now."

I looked at the piece of paper I had about the Lutey curse. We could command those to do good deeds. I guess the truth was her good deed.

"So answer," I sneered at Calliope.

"I gave you the comb so that you would find your way to your mother and the rest of your family. I'm glad you used it."

"So you lied to them!" My father was enraged. "I'm not sure why you kids were trusting this creature anyway."

In that moment I knew that we hadn't trusted her fully, but we were clinging to some hope that she was going to help us save our mom.

"I never lied to them. Ever. We only ever get to see fractions of the truth."

I broke free from Spencer and lashed out at Calliope. "I'm going to show you a fraction of my truth." I was quickly within reach and grabbed some feathers and plucked them right out of her feathered arm.

She had her hand up and was poised to do something to me, but Morgan spoke. "I command you to sit and tell us everything you know. Do not harm my sister." Calliope looked like she was entering a trance. She stepped away from me and sat down.

"Your mother is waiting for you in the spot they call the shark sanctuary. She remembers you and is trying to make her way home to all of you. She is trying to choose to be with your father and your family."

"How do we rescue her?"

"If you can bring her from the water and return her to land, she can remain on land."

I piped up, wondering about all of the health problems she had endured. "Will she be sick here on land?" I was worried about the answer.

"No, now that she knows who she is and is making a natural choice, she will be fine if she avoids certain land items and practices."

The room was filled with excited hopeful energy. This was the first bit of good news we'd had since she went overboard during the eclipse. Spencer put his hand in mine and squeezed lightly. He seemed less elated than everyone else.

"Let's get going then, before it's too dark."

"And what about Morgan?" my father asked Calliope, but she didn't respond, so I asked the question, trying to emulate Morgan's style as before.

"I command you to tell me if Morgan is going to be okay."

Calliope looked at me with a smirk. "I don't know. But I can tell you that Colin is on the island near the place where your mother is waiting for you. I've told you all that I know." She then held out the book that she was thumbing through when she first sat down and vanished.

I pulled my hand away from Spencer's hand. The page was all about the blue men of the Muir. They were the most powerful storm creators in the ocean. It was a very rare thing in the merperson world to be born into their line. They would add a brother to their clan about every hundred years and once in a blue moon. I had never heard that expression used that way before. The blue moon was an additional full moon—not expected. I walked out onto the balcony and looked up into the sky. Then I checked my phone for the phase of the moon. Another freaking full moon was on its way.

Morgan got close. "Muri, I know you can bring Mom home. I know it." He gave me the sweetest kiss on my forehead and then messed up my hair. "Remember, I will always be here to give you a hard time." Then he started talking directly to my heart, silently. I could feel his pure love for me and extreme fear about what was happening to his body. He was changing, so different from the fog of puberty that he was already experiencing. It was like his brain was rewiring and his senses were changing. He hugged me again and began to weep. "I'm scared, Muri."

My eyes filled with tears, and I could feel the pounding headache. It was the migraine that comes from holding back the floodgates of emotion. I didn't want to leave him. I couldn't leave him. My soul and entire being were linked to his existence. He made me relevant. I was a twin. He was my twin brother, a half that I should never be without. Yet, I had to go. I needed to find our mother. As I pulled away from him, I wanted to reassure him, but I couldn't. "Stay put. Stay away from the water. We'll be back with Mom."

Spencer tried to lighten the mood. "We'll all be fine. Order tons more food, watch every crazy movie on TV, and play video games. You won't even know we're gone."

Morgan walked back onto the patio and looked out toward the water. Dad motioned for me to go. Spencer and I headed out to meet our contact.

We walked in silence to the dock. The sky looked strange. It was telling the story of a storm that was coming, not one that had passed.

Father Lutey and Michael were waiting for us when we got to the dock. "You?"

"I'm here to help. Your uncle called Michael."

"How can you help us?" Spencer and I asked in unison.

Michael spoke up. "I told you that I worked in the military program training dolphins and sea lions. Well, some of those dolphins made their way here to the San Juan Islands after I freed them. That's the main reason why I'm no longer in the military and why I'm working at this parish. I think they'll do much better than any of us in locating a missing or captive person underwater. "I also have this." Father Lutey held up an ancient-looking letter opener. "I thought it might come in handy. It's not quite a knife, but it's pure meteoric iron, a gift from a Tibetan monk." He held it closer to us so that we could get a closer look at the ancient carvings on the side. It was of a mermaid. "This is Suvannamaccha, an Asian mermaid princess."

Father Lutey put the letter opener into a wooden sheath that was covered with other carvings that were difficult to decipher. He then handed it to me. "I hope you get your mother back. Let Michael do what he can to help."

"I have a boat and a score to settle with Colin," Michael added.

The NOAA boat was waiting for us. It was part of NOAA's small boat fleet. They kept around 400 boats around the country ready to deploy in near-shore operations. Some of the larger boats could also take extended deep-water trips. We were boarding a 26-foot boat equipped with sonar, dive gear, kayaks, and medical equipment. Michael dropped some sort of signal bait in the water, and Spencer and I put on scuba gear. It had been mere hours since we had left these same waters, but everything looked different. The sun was low in the sky, and the moon was trying to make its presence known. The shoreline was disheveled, trees were uprooted, and crabs were trying to scurry and dig new homes. We were on our way to Lopez Island and its Shark Reef. The water rippled slightly with sea life coming up for air.

Michael broke the silence. "We haven't seen a shark in Shark Reef for over a decade. The orca pods keep them out of the San Juan Islands. These orcas will eat a great white for dinner!" Spencer could tell I was nervous about the shark talk. I was glad that this wasn't their regular place to converge. I wasn't sure how fast word got around under the sea, but I knew I was no friend of the sharks after helping Bo. I hoped it was something I'd never have to think about again. He held my hand and I dialed Morgan. We still had a bit of cell reception. Dad picked up instead of Morgan.

"How's he doing?" Spencer asked. He was about to put the phone on speaker so we could talk to Morgan together, but something made him stop. He dropped the phone to the floor of the boat. I didn't feel anything from Morgan that suggested anything was wrong, so I wondered why Spencer was so wide-eyed. He sat down in the bottom of the boat, and I went to his side.

"What's going on?" I asked, still sure that Morgan was fine.

"Morgan decided to come after us. Colin was waiting for him and they dumped him in the harbor. Your Dad saw Morgan sink and never surface."

I didn't know what to feel—panic maybe, but I was sure he was okay. Michael dropped anchor as we reached the spot known as the shark sanctuary.

"We have to stay focused, one mission at a time. We can't do anything about what happened at the harbor." He then leaned over the side of the boat and slapped the side of it. Three bottlenose dolphins appeared. They squeaked and chirped at Michael. He petted each one of them and gave them a hand signal to submerge, then quickly jumped in the water with them. He had the sonar running. We could see the dolphins and Michael on his equipment. I had to believe that Spencer was mistaken. Morgan might have gotten away. I still didn't feel like he was in trouble. I believed in our connection. The storm clouds converged overhead, and it started to rain. Spencer and I slid into the water with all of our gear. Michael grabbed a couple of fishing spears on deck and handed one to me and one to Spencer.

We followed the dolphins, and they led us to the entrance of a series of underwater caves that extended beneath Lopez Island. The entrances were hidden by tall sea grasses and coral near seemingly impassible jagged rocks forming the undersea mounts. Michael fixed battery-operated lights to the flippers of the dolphins—they were our beacons in the gloomy abyss. The sky was dark and so was the sea. The water was even colder now that it was missing the sun. One of the dolphins circled back and swam behind me. The dolphin's position illuminated not just what was up ahead, but our group and everything on the periphery.

Spencer was the first to notice that we weren't alone. Dozens of eyes watched us as we passed. Fish, sea lions, sea turtles, harbor porpoises, and a frightening orca whale or two observed as we swam by. There was no apex predator here—no circle of life. They were waiting for the main event. They seemed to know that this wasn't their battle, but I felt like they were on our side if they had one.

We made a sharp turn and found ourselves deeper in the network of caves. I suddenly remembered that I was claustrophobic, something that I had inherited from my father. My heart was pounding in my ears, and I was grateful for the steady stream of oxygen that was being sent to me from my small tank. I didn't know how we would find our way back. I was hoping someone was leaving bread crumbs behind or something. Light was coming from an area at the end of what seemed to be a tunnel. No animals on the sidelines, just rock. As we swam further into the tunnel, the water receded. There was a surface. We followed the light and emerged in a pool in the center of a rock formation. It was like a hollowed-out volcano reaching all the way up to the sky. I was relieved by the open space. I could see Spencer was struggling as well. He pulled his mask off the moment he saw the fresh air. One by one, we all emerged into the moonlight. And then I saw her.

My mother was at the opposite end of the pool, watching us enter. Everything about her had changed since I had encountered her in the cove. Her long, curly black hair had gold flecks in it, with pink and purple seahorses holding pieces of her hair out of her face. As a piece of hair would catch movement, the seahorse would fasten it in place. She was adorned with pearls and a gold crown with spiky yellow crystals and purple geodes. Her skin shimmered with flecks of gold, and her tail was more gold than orange. It was as if Midas had kissed my mother and she was touched with just a bit of gold, infused throughout her entire body. Her eyes were different, human; the dark seal eyes were no more.

"Mom, Lorelei, are you ready to go back to land?" I swam a little closer to her and she backed up.

"Who are you?" she asked Spencer. I took this as a good sign that she knew who I was, directing her question at Spencer.

"I'm a friend of your husband and your children."

She looked around and asked me, "Where is Morgan?"

"I don't know. Colin pushed him into the harbor." I swam closer to her. She didn't move. Instead, she made several clicks and squeaks. Our companion dolphins came to the surface and responded to her. She made several more noises and then waved her hand. The dolphins dove and left the pool. I started to panic. "Mom—we needed those guys to get out of here."

My mom saw that I was in a panic. She remembered me. She knew me. She opened her arms, and I swam to her. Her body was silky in some spots and scaly in others. She held me close.

"I've sent them to search for your brother." Her voice sounded more like music than a voice when she talked to me.

"Mom, you can come home. Do you want to come home?" She looked at me and stroked my hair.

"Of course, my sweetheart. I want to come home. But it's not so easy." She turned and pressed her hand to a spot on the wall that glowed and opened a hidden passage to the city I had seen in the mirror. I was in awe as she revealed the entrance. She read my thoughts and responded, but to all three of us.

"We have been on this earth as long as anyone. We have technology, medicine, and magic. Why would man evolve and we would not? Only Muriel may enter here."

"Mom, I don't want to go in there. I want you to come with us. Let's get out of here." As I said this, two mermaids swam out of the portal she opened. They bowed their heads to my mother slightly before they spoke. I couldn't tell if this was a courteous custom or if my mother had some authority over them. Both of the mermaids had splotches on their skin—some type of hyperpigmentation. They seemed more like fish than my mother did. They also both had mossy-looking hair. The main difference they had between each other were their tails: one was coral colored and the other was teal.

The mermaid with the coral tail did the speaking: "The storm and the first wave coming to destroy is heading toward the Huai River in China. It will take this most polluted water and envelop the cancer villages."

I wasn't sure if they were calling the people in the village a cancer that needed to be gotten rid of or something else. Again, my mother read my thoughts.

"These are villages along the river with hundreds of people left to die of cancer. Their water is extremely polluted. There are no fish left; it's just toxic waste." Then she turned and spoke to the mermaid. "I see why the believers would start there. They can promote their cause by saying they are choosing to help those abandoned humans out of their misery and cleanse the waters. How are they attempting this, since we are not helping them?"

"They located the last piece of the prophecy. He is a very powerful blue man of the Muir." The minute she said this I thought about Morgan, and my mother instantly knew what we all did. Morgan was their blue man.

"Let's go, Mom." I yearned for her to return home and to our lives.

"I have cherished you always, every moment." She leaned in and kissed me with a sweet and gentle goodbye. Her seahorses wept for her. They hid in her hair since they, too, knew her heart. She then whispered to me, "Take care of your father." I heard this but wasn't processing it all.

Spencer aimed his fishing spear at her.

"You should come back with Muriel. She needs you."

The two mermaids swam quickly behind my mother and raised their bodies out of the water. Their hair expanded and they seemed twice as large as they had just a moment ago. They hissed and had fang-like teeth. They either were coming to my mother's protection or were her captors. I wasn't sure of the dynamics of their relationship.

I produced the letter opener and moved toward the mermaids. My mother raised her hand, and the mermaids retreated.

"Muriel, what are you doing?" she asked calmly.

"You're coming home with us. It was a mistake that you are even here. You need to come home with us."

Spencer was shaky with his spear.

My mother turned toward me. "I'm sorry, Muri. I can't go with you back home. Not yet. I have to find Morgan." She pleaded with me to understand, but I couldn't.

"No. You don't know what you're saying. We'll find Morgan, too. It will be okay. You're coming home with us. We have a boat."

The dolphins returned and nudged at me, then made clicks and squeaks to the mermaid Lorelei.

"We have to get moving. There is some sort of danger out there. They are urging you to go," my mother told us.

"Your brother is under Colin's control. He is creating a storm on this coast right now."

I heard these words from my mother, but they didn't mean any-thing to me. Was she choosing Morgan over coming home and all of us working together to bring him home? I started to feel twitchy and alone. I continued to point the letter opener at my mother and her mermaid companions. She was coming with us. I wasn't going to lose her again.

I was starting to feel the electricity pulse through my body again. I could feel the fear and anger rising in me. My mom was coming home with me whether she thought it was a good idea or not. My mother nodded her head and spoke to the dolphins with a squeak.

"Follow these dolphins out of here before the storm outside is impassable. Muriel, your choices are to come with me into the city or go back with your father, but I cannot join you." I looked at her in disbelief and took on the role of a petulant child.

"No, your choice is to come with us and that's it." The electricity buzzed around me. She looked at me sternly but spoke in the voice I remembered from childhood. The one that helped me tame my emotions, use my words, and see the bigger picture.

"Muri, do you want to hurt Spencer and any other humans in the water? If you continue with what you are doing, that small current that surrounds you now will engulf this whole pool. I see your thoughts, and you remember what it did to Morgan." As she spoke, I became aware of the buzzing around my body. I started to cry.

"Please choose us, Mom. Please choose me. We'll find Morgan. We can all do it together." She then spoke directly to me through my thoughts.

"I will always choose you, my sweet. You are loved beyond measure. I see your gifts and your burdens, but my destiny is elsewhere. Let me go. Your brother needs me. There is a friend waiting for you with the sharks. He knows where we are going." She moved toward me. I put my spear down and she started to pass me and head to the entrance of the hidden mermaid city.

"No!" I screamed. "You're not doing this." I fired my fishing spear by accident and grazed Spencer. His blood trickled into the water. My mother and the other mermaids rushed to his aid. My mother emitted an electric pulse like the current I was spreading through the water, but hers was targeted at Spencer's wound. It sealed his wound slightly.

"You must take him to the surface as quickly as you can. We can do no more for him." A mermaid harnessed Spencer to one of the dolphins with sea grass. I was compelled to hold on to the dolphin as well, and we glided out of the sea caves.

I heard my mother whispering in my ear, "Go, go my sweet." As if in a trance, I looked up to the sky and saw a lunar rainbow (a moonbow). I was still and listened as the chaos swirled around me. There was spray and splatter as our diving party tried to escape to safety, but I was frozen—listening. Then I heard it. It was Morgan's calm voice: "Find me." I watched my mother move through the gates to the hidden mermaid city.

I moved swiftly toward the edge of this realm. At the entrance to the caves we saw the trouble. Sharks. Dozens of sharks, waiting for me. I heard a whimpering and a muffled cry coming from one of them. It had something in its mouth: a strange glistening fish, Bo.

I heard Morgan's voice again: "Find me." Spencer was losing blood in the water. The sharks smirked and blocked the dolphin from carrying us any further. The storm above swirled but was digging in deeper and creating circles of currents kicking up sand and vegetation. The sharp, disturbing underwater elements being swirled scraped against me, irritating my senses. The loud noises of the whimpers, thoughts, sharks, Spencer, my mother, Morgan whispering to me... Find me.... Buzzing, buzzing, buzzing... my father, humming, chanting, Colin, Morgan whispering to me.... Find me, Spencer calling out as a shark lashed out at the dolphin. . . J pod orcas wailing. . . Morgan once more calling to me: Find me! Buzzing.... Buzzing....

I closed my eyes and prayed, "Thy will be done." Electricity pulsed with every beat of my heart and pulsed outward in rhythmic blasts until everything was silent and floating, including me. What remained was total darkness and silence. Then there was a flash and whispering from Bo. His voice was all I could hear. "Your brother and mother are in the waters of the Minch. They have gone to the Western Isles." Then darkness and silence again, another flash, and a moment where I knew Spencer and I were dragged to the surface by divers. That was my last memory until I woke a month later in a house that had never had a brother or a mother living there. Some wishes do come true. I was no longer a twin.